Lostlindens

Lostlindens

A FULL ACCOUNT; WITH NEW INFORMATION CONCERNING THE RIDDLE OF SHAKESPEARE'S BOOT

AN IVORY TOWER MYSTERY

DAVID D. NOLTA

QUALITY WORDS IN PRINT

Q W P

Lostlindens
An Ivory Tower Mystery

Copyright © 2005 David D. Nolta
Published by Quality Words In Print, LLC
P. O. Box 2704, Costa Mesa, California 92628-2704
www.qwipbooks.com

Cover and Interior Design by Desktop Miracles, Inc.

First Edition

Printed in the United States of America

Library of Congress Cataloging-in-Publication Data

Nolta, David Derbin.
    Lostlindens : an ivory tower mystery / David D.
Nolta.
       p. cm.
    ISBN 0-9713160-5-8
    1. Americans—England—Fiction. 2. College
students—Crimes against—Fiction. 3. Brothers
and sisters—Fiction. 4. College teachers—Fiction.
5. Country homes—Fiction. 6. England—Fiction.
I. Title.
PS3614.O48L67   2005   813'.6—dc22
                                  2004004540

For the meek swain and for his joy-creating bride;
  For sweet Jane and her gentle, loving spouse;
For Lon, Moose, Dom and the Angel who cried—
  Each of whose kindness is a kind of country house.

I

ENGLISH LIFE IN LITERATURE

(Wherein many names are introduced,
but no worry as to remembering them)

W HEN ONE PICTURES THE ENGLISH COUNTRYSIDE, a variety of usually pleasing scenes come to mind. Among these, the traffic jam rarely figures. For some unreasonable reason, traffic jams, like violent crimes and chemically-preserved foods, seem more in keeping with general notions of ex-colonial, and especially American, life than that of the Mother Country. Nevertheless, the little white coach trying to make what ought to be the brief journey from Central London to Cambridgeshire, under a bright sky that also seemed more American than British in its breadth and depth and the unmitigated blueness of its awning, was most definitely stuck in traffic. It had moved hardly more than a few inches during the past forty minutes, after which interval the driver, a frugal Scot, had at last switched the engine off.

Inside the little bus, several of the occupants had expressed, according to their respective tolerance levels and temperaments, their dismay at this latest hitch in the proceedings, though all but two were American and so quite used to blockages of this sort. Then they had become bored with the problem and even with the pleasure of complaining, and one by one, or sometimes in pairs, they had all fallen to sleep, lulled by or in spite of the great noises which rocked their caravan on either side. Among these, Whitney Houston's high-pitched plea for information, "How will I know if he really loves me?" emanating from the open-topped sports car to the east of the little white coach, was answered, if inappositely, by the less loud but no less impassioned or solipsistic speculations of Marguerite's *"Il m'aime. Il ne m'aime pas"* from Gounod's *Faust*, ribboning through a gap in the window of the BMW on the western side. And inside the bus, Mr. MacMenzies—pronounced, as he insisted, Mic MING hees—kept the portable radio, held with rubber bands to the dashboard, tuned to something more indicative of his own heritage and tastes: a bagpipe rendition of ancient Highland airs.

To all of these sounds, the sleepers were by now oblivious. As participants in a six-week program ambitiously entitled *English Life in Literature*, they had been constantly on the move for the past twenty days. The greatest part of that period they had spent in London, at the quietest of times an exhausting city which can break even the most leisurely of travelers. This particular group comprised not tourists, but twelve college students and their two instructors who had undertaken a definitive examination of every aspect of English life as that has been portrayed or, as some prefer, invented by the greatest English writers from the sixteenth century to the present day. "But can you really come to any conclusions about national life, about the evolving life of a people, even restricting yourself to its description in key literary works, in a month and a half?" This query, posed only two days into the course by the least consistently voluble of the students, a young man named Michael Teller, had been greeted with patriotic suspicion by the other members of the group. "Of course it can be done. We are Americans, after all." Such was the general appetite and enthusiasm prevailing throughout the first week of the program.

And so they had set out to prove their point and seemed well on their way to succeeding. A typical day, for example, June 23rd, passed in the following manner: At seven-thirty in the morning, after a quick breakfast in their Bloomsbury hotel, the group toured the area around Fitzroy and Gordon Squares, rife with the restless spirits of the famously talented, amoral, but inevitably genteel friends and followers of the Woolfs and the Bells. Then, moving roughly northwest on the map and backward in time, the group arrived at Hampstead Heath, for a quick visit to the house where John Keats came down with tuberculosis. Lunch, consisting of Marks and Spencer's sandwiches, was eaten *en route* to Westminster Abbey, where a relatively relaxed half hour was spent sorting out those poets who are actually buried in Poets' Corner from the far greater number of those merely commemorated there—a revelation of disproportion which disappointed certain of the students, and against which several of them, feeling vaguely that they had been overcharged, rebelled. After the Abbey and a six-minute lavatory stop, they reassembled to make their way on foot to a two-o'clock matinee performance of Wycherly's *Country Wife* at the St. James Theatre, a play which, to judge from the reaction of one student, Kimberly Ann Crestview of Baltimore, still has the power to scandalize and discompose. After the play, another walk brought them to Rose Street, formerly Rose Alley, and Will's Coffee House, where Lord Rochester had Dryden ambushed and where each student was allowed one glass of sherry, the choice of dry or sweet being left to the individual.

Finally, after a meal at Kettner's, Oscar Wilde's favorite restaurant now owned by a pizza chain, there was just time for the group to make the eight-o'clock curtain of *Titus Andronicus* at the Theatre Royal Haymarket. Thankfully, perhaps, most of the students were asleep long before the child-serving scene.

And so sleep, in any posture, at any empty moment of the day, became the visual leitmotif of the scholarly progress. Even the two supervisors of the course had given in to it now. One, an Englishman named Anthony Trefthven-Woooser, was snoring blandly into his inflatable headrest, a recognizably un-English accessory which had in fact been given to him by one of his new American admirers, a girl named Paula Simon. Anthony, or Tony as he preferred, lounged awkwardly in the first seat behind the driver. With his long, grey-trousered left leg folded underneath him, and his long fingers splayed across the sienna of his custom-made shirt and his leaf-green tie, he gave the impression of an insect, a mantis or a walking stick, which had fallen from its tree and which had soon realized the futility of trying to camouflage itself in such unnatural surroundings—far easier just to play dead. It was his head rather than his lanky extremities which had been the source of Tony's appeal among the students in his charge. At thirty-six, he had a boyish face with a proverbial English complexion and an ebullient mane of prematurely silvering hair which projected impressively against the blue plastic pillow.

Immediately behind him was the admiring provider of the Aid to Rest, Paula Simon. She, too, territorially claimed both seats in her row. At twenty-one and a half, and as a graduating senior, Miss Simon represented the mature guard in this small academic expeditionary force, and she herself was forever conscious of her role as a wiser and more experienced member of the troop, something of a self-appointed subaltern to the two captains in command. Almost as though to make up for her relative sophistication and the greater seriousness of her intellectual goals, she was characteristically late for class *rendez-vous* and gave a general impression of disorganization which undermined somewhat the authority she felt was her due. A medium-sized young woman with long blond hair and a protective smile, she was well spoken but generally quiet, sometimes to the point of seeming furtive. For example, at the very moment that we have come upon her, she was only half asleep, keeping one eye on the silver head that overlapped the seat in front of her and both ears forever attuned to any potentially meaningful sounds rising from among the other eleven students dispersed behind her.

With regard to these eleven companions, sleeping as soundly as did the same number of Apostles after

the Last Supper, the reader is perhaps already anticipating a series of concise character descriptions along
the lines of those provided for Miss Simon and the
young English don who was the object of her growing interest. And in this premonition, the reader is
correct. But, speaking as the writer, I feel that some
sort of preliminary apology may be in order. You see,
I myself read somewhere recently that an author, or
anyone who recounts the details of a story, should
never blatantly describe the characters who make up
that story; that the author's responsibility is merely
to make the briefest of introductions, and then to let
the characters identify themselves. This seems like a
sound precept, on the whole; however, I find that,
being an overly curious person, and preoccupied as
I am with the silent and invisible facets of human
personality—as well as due to my commitment to
contextualizing as truthfully as possible, by way of
making some reference to the past which falls outside of my narrative, the actual incidents which are
its substance—I must have my short say about each
of them before we begin. After all, however interesting people may be, what we think about them is of
even greater interest to us. Furthermore, if we waited
for certain characters to describe or reveal themselves
by their actions, we must needs wait indefinitely, to
use an old-fashioned phrase. So, with your permission

and with my thanks, we will continue with this brief but essential *Dramatis Personae*.

Directly behind Paula Simon was a young man named Rupert Augustus. True to the Prussian ring of his name, he was tall, blond, solidly built, with a vaguely military air and a facial expression or inexpression far beyond what is required for inscrutability. If Rupert had had his way, he would have been at the very head of the coach, or even driving it. He had considered doing whatever was necessary to occupy the foremost seat, including pushing or pulling Paula out of his path as she hastily boarded the bus. But there were too many people watching for him to perform so blatantly ungentlemanly an act. Conceding a temporary defeat, he had authoritatively positioned himself behind her, and subsequently fallen asleep like the rest of the students, though the position he maintained, sitting bolt upright the way Alcantarines occupy their narrow tombs, was perhaps the oddest of all. And, like the deceased of any order, he seemed to produce a soundlessness as inarguable and rigid as his posture.

As though out of deference or fear, the seat directly behind Rupert Augustus was empty, but the next down contained two sophomore women whose complimentarily inclined bodies formed a perfect pyramid of repose. Sarah Magister and Mame

Freeline had not known each other before beginning this course, but shortly thereafter they had become fast and eternal friends. What brought them together was the singular quality they shared, namely, self-sufficiency, an independence which, though common to both, manifested itself in each of them in decidedly different ways. Sarah was the more introspective of the two; with her very curly, very long, light brown hair and her huge brown eyes, she had an angelic, inviolably complacent look. Except with her closest friends, who now included Mame, she was not given to chattiness, but when she did speak, her words usually conveyed reasonable and intelligent thoughts, these most often phrased as questions. Her questioning nature and her serious, wide-ranging interests sometimes rendered her pedantic, and she was also profoundly, though never loudly, critical, as well as hard to please. The dark-haired Mame, on the other hand, tended to be less serious in her scholarly pursuits and less demanding in her pleasures. Attractive and energetic and outgoing, Mame worked thirty hours a week as a waitress in order to pay for her education, and she never denied the fact that for her, *English Life in Literature* was at least as much a vacation as it was a course of study. Nevertheless, she was both bright and enthusiastic. Had she modeled for any of those Old Masters who loved to isolate and personify particular human traits, Mame would have cropped up in their iconography as the very image of "Savvy" or "Spunk," her attributes a closely clasped handbag and a compact video camera ready to record not only pretty views, but ambiguous situations that might demand clarification later on.

Michael Teller, whom we have already encountered, occupied alone the seat behind Sarah and Mame. Mike was a stereotypical bookworm, invariably reading except during the brief intervals spent considering what to read or re-read next. Like Sarah Magister, Mike was questioning and could be critical, but he was by far the shiest of all the students, and this showed in his appearance and his mannerisms, notable among the latter being a tendency to dip his bespectacled head when approached closely by one of his fellows, as though to duck from a blow. Occasionally, his shyness would give way to a sudden and, because of the long periods separating such moments, alarming indulgence in speech. At such times, he was like an unpredictable faucet that, successfully turned on, produces a forceful but unapproachable spray of water and requires a wrench to be shut off. But, as we have suggested, there was nothing forceful in his appearance. In fact, physically he was hardly noticeable, with short brown hair the exact color of his tortoise-shell glasses, a wide and enigmatically smiling mouth, and the very youthful air that is the only fringe benefit of the habitually bullied.

Finally, the last seat on Mr. Trefthven-Woooser's side of the bus was filled with Ruthie Slatt. Ruthie had a broad face like a billboard with no message, or at least not one that people were tempted to read, and the scattering of pimples she took no trouble to conceal, like the nose and lip piercings of which she was fiercely proud, only increased this projection of determined resistibility. So, in fact, the signboard did bear a message: Keep Off, a warning further borne out by her dress and posture. She wore a somewhat grimy tee shirt, several sizes too small, revealing in an aggressive and even frightening way an amorphous, hardly female torso, and large areas of her white ankles burst out below the overly short cuffs of her blue jeans, giving the impression that she had put these on at the age of twelve and then neglected to take them off as she got older, so that now it was no longer an option. She was rather wedged than sitting in her seat, with her broad behind hanging over the edge and her legs doubled up and braced against the seat-back in front of her; the illogicality of this position somehow suggested a ship in a bottle, or an extra large egg thaumaturgically fixed below the rim of an eggcup. Like her companions, she was asleep, but even in this state she preserved a defiant, if not minatory, aura; snoring quietly but somehow angrily, one assumed she must be arguing and possibly cursing in her dreams.

Except that they were all engaged in the serious study of English Life and Literature, the students brought together and now sleeping communally on the bus had in fact very little in common. There was, however, one thing upon which they had all come to agree: Ruthie was a pain. She was loud and bossy, her moods alternating unpredictably between morose irritability and bubbly, girlish talkativeness, neither of which attitudes rendered her appealing to her companions. Worst of all, she was given to the telling of apparently outrageous, self-glorying lies. The two supervisors, when they came, very early into the course, to disregard the details of her howlers, were somewhat impressed by Ruthie's command of language and the force of her delivery, but no such appreciative response filtered down among her peers, and it had taken surprisingly little time to establish once and for all her position as pariah, a distinction she herself found not altogether without prestige.

This general disaffection was definitively confirmed, and can be illustrated here, by an incident that occurred on the group's second evening in London. Having recovered from their jet lag, but not yet having been exhausted by the frantic pace of the course they

were just beginning, all the students had decided to
go scouting together for nightspots or dance parties
that might prove up to the high standard of American youth. This would be the only time the students
unanimously undertook anything unofficial—that
is to say, without being forced—but at this stage,
there still lingered among them a general feeling of
goodwill and that sense of mutual acceptance which
is the first thing to be sacrificed in prolonged and
unchanged company. Though not one of them had
been out of the United States before (it was in fact
the first time that two or three of them had been on
a plane), several of the students, including Ruthie,
had declared that they knew exactly where to go
for the most exciting time. As she was the loudest
and, clearly, the one most likely to prove problematic,
and perhaps physically violent, if crossed, she finally
had her way, leading the group on foot in the direction of Bayswater, talking the whole time in bright
and colorful language of how she had an uncle who
was a baronet (she spoke the word quickly, so that it
sounded somewhat agricultural), who was a regular
old-school rake and who had told her exactly where to
obtain the cheapest liquor, the trendiest drugs, and, if
you stuck with it, the wildest sexual partners. Some
of the students, including Sarah Magister and Mike
Teller, felt a clammy stiffness in their lower joints at

the mention of these enticements. But they all continued to follow their hefty leader, who became more gregarious and outgoing as they walked on, shouting occasionally to strangers and even giving a shove to a young man whom she judged to come too close on his bike, though it was she who was walking in the clearly-marked bicycle lane.

They walked for two hours, and by the end of that time, several of them were becoming restless, to say the least. They passed a couple of places that looked, if not promising, possible, but Ruthie would not relent, exhorting them, sometimes pleadingly and at other times brusquely, to trust her. By midnight, all they had come to was the realization that they did not trust her. In pairs or groups of three, they abandoned her for whatever clubs were on hand, and none of them made a pretense of inviting her along. An hour later, she was left alone, wandering an area which, in her own mind at any rate, she continued to insist she knew like the back of her hand. The fruitless journey was more than sufficient cause for the others to question their prior deference to her, and to vow not to indulge her in the future. But the night was still young. The real problems began when she returned, at around four o'clock in the morning, to the hotel.

The Covington was neither a dive nor a rival to Claridge's. It was an old, fairly safe establishment on the edge of Bloomsbury, after all still a highly fashionable part of town. And its group rates rendered it a favorite host to American academic programs and package theater tours, between which, needless to add, there is little detectable difference. Erected in the late nineteenth century in what we can term the "Regency Raj" style, its exterior was a calculating tribute to Brighton Pavilion, though on a much bigger scale. Inside, however, the public and private spaces had long since been remodeled, so that what had once been a comfortable bedroom was now six, each a double, and within every adjacent minaret were half a dozen disconcertingly triangular bathrooms.

In the lottery for roommates which had been the first order of business upon the group's arrival in London, Ruthie had drawn Paula Simon. Reasonable, rational, temperate, tolerant Paula had been asleep for some time when Ruthie returned to The Covington in the wee hours of the morning after her failed attempt at Pied Pipering. She opened the door of the tiny room, turned on the light, whacked her solid right ankle against her roommate's bed, and proceeded to introduce to a startled Miss Simon her new friend, also called Simon, Simon Lang, recently of Newcastle-upon-Tyne. Paula was not intentionally querulous when she responded with a simple "Excuse me?", politely pulling the covers up around her face.

Ruthie's voice, however, was already gathering the momentum of an as-yet uninitiated argument when she explained the situation to Paula.

"I know you won't mind if Simon sleeps here tonight. It's only for a couple hours, but he's locked himself out of his flat, and he's already in trouble with the landlord, so he can't wake him up at this hour. I never said I wouldn't be bringing friends back—they never told us we couldn't. Besides, there's plenty of room. It's only for one night. I told him you'd be cool."

Simon, a tall, unwashed twenty-year-old with holes in the knees of his tight trousers, looked puzzled when Ruthie mentioned the word landlord, but his bewilderment was swiftly transformed into admiration for her inventive intelligence. He leaned back against the wall—there was no place else for him to go unless he crawled over Paula in her bed—and lit a cigarette. Paula, who was not yet wide awake, reacted instantly and with uncharacteristic emotion to the strange situation being thrust upon her, emitting a little scream. This surprised the interloping Lang, not altogether awake himself. He dropped his cigarette, which ignited an astonishingly large area of polyurethane carpet near his feet. Paula screamed again, jumping from the bed to get water from the sink, in which she was assisted by the newcomer, while Ruthie looked on with slight amazement at the

sudden blaze. She was momentarily excited by the dis-
traction it caused, but wanted it put out as soon as
possible so that she could take up again the argument
that she had correctly foreseen would arise if she tried
to smuggle someone into her room.

Seconds later, when she had successfully doused
the superficial fire, an ashen Paula spoke out with
steely calm.

"Ruthie, it's four in the morning. I'm going back
to bed. You may not bring a guest into the room—that
is no way to treat me. I'm sorry, Mr. Lang, but you
have to go, and if there's any problem, I'm going to
call the front desk."

Something—and possibly more than one thing—
in Paula's tone made it resoundingly clear that she
would not be gainsaid. After letting out a loud huff,
Ruthie slammed her backpack down on the new burn-
mark on the floor, and, grabbing her friend by the
sleeve, acknowledged her defeat with a single word,
"Fine!", before the two of them left, Mr. Lang lighting
another cigarette and politely bowing his head on the
way out.

Never one to give up easily, Ruthie took her newfound friend and went knocking at the doors of each
of the other students in the program, whispering
apologetically that her old friend Simon (he became
her sick cousin in the final version) needed a place to

spend the night. Each of the irritated people she awak-
ened in turn responded emphatically in the negative,
Mame Freeline even threatening to rouse the instructors. Furious, Ruthie was finally forced to send Simon
Lang back to his nonexistent landlord. And so it was
a double alienation that Ruthie had effected from all
of her peers that second night of the program.

Curiously, Paula Simon bore Ruthie no particular
grudge after the incident of the fire, but the others
had rallied increasingly against her, and lurid tales of
her daily behavior were dispensed at meal times and,
later, in smoky, sequestered drinking establishments
far from The Covington's paper-thin walls. Now, on
the bus, she popped unwelcome into several of their
dreams, and they worried unconsciously that she
might be with them long after the program ended.

One of the people whose slumber was currently thus
fretted was sitting in the opposite corner from Ruthie
at the back of the coach. Kimberly Ann Crestview was
a distinguished sophomore, a prominent member of the
better of the two vestigial sororities on campus back in
Illinois, as well as the real power behind the mentally
incompetent president of the women's glee club there.
More recently, she had become the self-appointed
leader of the anti-Ruthie movement.

As already noted, Kimberly Ann—she always
used both names—was from Baltimore, and she bore

this middle Atlantic heritage like a heavy tiara on her weary but unwavering brow. Though technically from a border territory, she was a Southerner to the core: by birth, as she felt herself, and by inclination, as anyone who met her soon came to realize. Her manners, perhaps better described as her affectations, seemed based upon excessive study of Margaret Mitchell enhanced by a willful misreading of Tennessee Williams. Similarly, her wardrobe consisted without exception of lightweight, virginal pastels more appropriate to tea parties on plantation lawns than trudging through the rainy streets of central London or the dusty chambers of the Tower, the latter of which she silently censured for being unpapered. A large-boned, bushy blonde, she never walked but she swept, never looked but she gazed, and most of her gazes ended in a disapproving frown.

Unlike her native state during the Civil War, Kimberly Ann had no mixed feelings or self-contradicting principles; she was not torn, she was sure. And since the first hours of this course, she had been most sure of one thing, that she must never relent in her persecution of the young woman whose diametric antithesis she desperately hoped people recognized her to be: Ruthie Slatt. No doubt Kimberly Ann expended unnecessary energy in order to enhance the contrast with Ruthie, as certainly, in most superficial respects, the two had little enough in common. Kimberly Ann didn't really look anything like Ruthie—she was sure of that. She was considerably slimmer, though not as much slimmer as she would wish to have been. She wore make-up, and Ruthie Slatt clearly wouldn't know which end of the concealment stick to use—in fact, thought Kimberly Ann, she'd probably swallow it whole. Furthermore, Ruthie was ill-dressed, ill-mannered, and aggressive without ever being merely outgoing, her speech often coarse, and sometimes downright dirty. Kimberly Ann, on the other hand, was studiously if not altogether effectively charming, prudish in mind, and delicate in expression. And yet, they might, for all that, have been sisters, or at least cousins. This horrible realization of an affinity between the two girls was brought painfully home to Kimberly Ann before the plane had even left the airport in Chicago.

Though all of the students had already gotten to know one another at the various organizational meetings held in advance of the course, at the earliest of which Kimberly Ann had taken an instant, automatic, but not very detailed, dislike to Ruthie, it was only when they boarded the plane that she was forced to consider the grotesque possibility that there might exist some link between them, if only in other people's minds. Kimberly Ann had just loaded the third and last of her matching carry-on bags—this one filled to bursting with electric beauty aids, individually packaged, pre-moistened towelettes, and an iron—into the overhead compartment. She was easing herself into her seat, gracefully rescuing the headset from beneath her left buttock, when she heard the two male students sitting directly ahead uninhibitedly exchanging views on the female element of the group.

"Yeah, she's okay, I guess," said Herman Wadkin, a good-looking football player for whom the merely okay held no attractions.

Curious as to whom they were assessing, Kimberly Ann leaned forward.

"How about Ruthie?" snickered the more aesthetically-oriented Paul Stripling. "She's a pill, eh?"

Behind them, Kimberly Ann smiled her agreement.

"Yeah, and that other one, the stuck-up one, Kimberly or Kelly or whatever her name is. She's just as bad. In fact, I keep getting them confused," confided Herman, all too audibly.

"Now that you mention it, I see what you mean," responded Paul, with a kind of awe at the palpably just comparison. "I mean, she's more dressed up and prickly and all, but they actually act a lot alike. Maybe they're sisters!"

"I'd hate to see the mother," said Herman soberly.

Kimberly Ann fell back in her seat. It was as though she had been discreetly stabbed by the passing stewardess. As though she had suddenly found herself before a mirror in a fairy tale, and a stern voice had called out, "This is the white trash version of you!" And there was Ruthie Slatt. The sudden, horrifying consciousness that other people might see them as being somehow alike destroyed her peace and scorched her soul. Even more searing was the possibility that being relative strangers, these two terrible men had spoken a profound and— God forbid!—a more generally held truth. It is a well-known fact that what we overhear about ourselves is far more dangerous than overt criticism, the barb of which is as often as not blunted by our knowledge or suspicion of the speaker's disingenuous desire to wound. Still, the idea was not merely preposterous, it was eviscerating, and the victim vowed immediately to make not the men, but Ruthie, pay.

Under normal circumstances, thrown together with strangers, it would be Kimberly Ann's *modus operandi* to reveal her superiority slowly and by hardly perceptible, feminine degrees. But how could she prove that she was the consummate product of generations of hothouse breeding, the perfect, most exquisite, hybrid rose, if she clearly resembled, in some minuscule but insurmountable respect, the stinkweed that was Ruthie Slatt?

Then and there, her mission became clear. She—
yes she, Kimberly Ann Crestview, elder daughter of
Harmon Peabody Crestview and Miranda Wilpool
Crestview Frink—would exert herself, would spare
no mental or psychological effort in putting Ruthie
Slatt in her proper place, so far below Kimberly Ann
that the Biblical distance between Lazarus and Dives
was nothing by compare. Kimberly Ann couldn't
remember clearly who was the nice man in that story,
but she knew that one of them landed in the lake of
fire, and that was exactly where she planned to send
Ruthie. Ironically enough from a moral standpoint,
this new determination of Kimberly Ann's brought
out a latent imagination, and an intellectual range
hitherto hardly to be associated with her. In her deal-
ings with Ruthie, she skipped back and forth between
blatant rudeness and what might be termed violent
indifference, a resolve to ignore the other woman that
seemed no less obvious than spitting at her would
have been. She played upon the ready flute of the
other's name an endless number of nasty variations.
She argued with her constantly on the pettiest of pre-
texts. She even relaxed her lofty pretensions among
the others in the group, with no single member of
whom she had anything worthwhile in common, in
order to give a broader base and greater impact to
the insult of her dismissal of Slatt. And worst of all,

on those rare occasions when they found themselves alone together, she merely laughed.

Ruthie, for her part, was at first taken off guard by these assaults, used as she was to being the aggressor at any gathering. Then she had worried that Kimberly Ann might be trying, in some perverse way, to be her friend. But finally she had seen the light, and struck back in kind. This had happened quite suddenly in London, during the intermission at a West End production of Noel Coward's *Design for Living*, when she had interrupted Kimberly Ann in the midst of one of the latter's cruel and unambiguous tirades by saying in a loud voice appropriate to the theater setting, "If you don't shut up, I'm going to stuff your mouth with more shit than they found on the battlefield of Antietam!" an astounding and, on the literal level, an idle and illogical threat, which nevertheless stopped the other dead in her tracks.

After this incident, what is popularly and more often than not optimistically described as a "conflict-resolution" meeting was held, under the direction of Mr. Trefthven-Woooser. As a result, the two women shifted gears, their mutual hatred buried, if only barely, under a horrible, hard-edged bonhomie. Meanwhile the presence of Ruthie was like a mite laying ever more eggs under Kimberly Ann's skin. Now, sleeping at the back of the bus, they communicated all the evenly-balanced ferocity of two demons guarding the emergency exit, beyond which was a whole world less frantically preoccupied with the search for comprehensive enlightenment on the topic of English life in literature.

If Kimberly Ann was still tormented by the suggestion that had instigated her personal crusade against Ruthie, namely, that most of the group thought they were alike, she need not have worried, for most of the group had already moved on to other, more pressing concerns, and, except during the aforementioned, necessarily well-spaced, gossip sessions, never willingly thought of them at all. The proof of this was spread over the next three seats in front of Kimberly Ann. Paul Stripling sat in the first of these, sleep throwing over his youthful countenance a smooth, unwrinkled veil. At this moment he resembled Endymion, or, with his somewhat narrow face ending in a light, almost linear beard, one of those Coptic portraits which still stare wonderingly at the passing ages from museum walls. And as with those ancient likenesses, painted after all in encaustic, there was something waxen about Paul's appearance, youthful and unblemished as that was. It was as though what one saw of him was not, in fact, natural, but rather an artistic result far greater than anything Kimberly Ann could produce with all the hues and ingenuity

her mind and makeup could supply. Paul was studious, though not as studious as Michael Teller, nor
merely in the sense of being bookish. He studied
also how to make himself pleasing to people, so that,
Endymion or no, there was something of the sales-
man about him as well. This is by no means unusual
even in the young, but in Paul's case, it seemed to
be the source of a vague anxiety, hardly noticeable
except in the rarest of social circumstances.

Paul was seemingly relaxed and comfortable in
the company of the robust, athletic Herman Wadkin who sat one seat ahead on the coach. If Mame
was Spunk, then here was Vigor. Mr. Wadkin, at
twenty years old, had won more trophies for running
and jumping and flinging himself about and knocking other people down than even his doting mother
could keep dusted, so she had had to box them the
very morning after her son's departure to take up his
football scholarship in Illinois. The Wadkins were, by
all accounts, regular, simple Midwestern folk, and it
was Herman's exceptional simplicity that had made
it possible for him to enroll in this course. In short,
he had failed three English classes in two years. The
football coach, who could not risk losing his favorite
tackle due to inadequate grades, had actually found
the money to pay for Herman's experience abroad in a
special, discretionary fund normally reserved for team

recruitments and all-night victory celebrations. Coach Williams, who had a vague notion that foreign study would be less rigorous and more in keeping with Herman's easygoing, extracurricular way of life back on campus, was happy to make the transaction as a last-ditch effort to rescue his young player from academic suspension. If this description seems a bit unfair, it is important to remember that Herman had his better points, too. With his neatly trimmed black hair, his blue eyes, his perfect skin and teeth and form, he was as good-looking as it is possible for a young man to be without ever giving the impression of being a thinking person. Furthermore, he had a sense of fair play, and was scrupulously polite, especially to his elders. And when he chose, he could be charming, even humorous in a monosyllabic sort of way.

Herman was the large centerpiece, the gorgeous, gilt-bronze clock with a pleasant face hiding a hardly-working mechanism, in a garniture of which Paul Stripling was one candelabrum, and the other was a young woman named Molly Version. Sitting just ahead of Herman, Molly was the youngest and most energetic student on the course. She was also, by her own admission, a man-eater, and just eighteen! Fresh-person Molly had green eyes and long brown hair and she was always smiling, and her smiles were never ambiguous, but overtly hungry—for life, for love, and above all for pleasure. Though she was bigger and better-proportioned and altogether more voluptuous than the most famous images of Eve by Cranach and Masaccio, she still had more than a little of the primal, persuasive female about her. But if Molly Version had been in the Garden of Eden, she would have had no qualms about the repercussions of her actions, devouring greedily as much of the forbidden fruit as she could get her hands on in the limited time allowed. Nor would a single Adam ever have sufficed. Right now, she was torn in her attraction to both Paul and Herman, each of whom seemed to like her in his own way. And so this group of three could always be found conjoined, as it were, by their overlapping and complementary interests in one another, and at this stage, it would have been unthinkable that any two of them should have shared a single seat, thereby insensitively forcing the third to sit alone. So they moved through London, and now through the English countryside, in what was to all appearances a balanced and contented row.

Just beyond this happy trio sat the only bona fide couple in the group, Saul Raven and Libby Moss. Saul was a gangly, long-haired blond in black leather pants, and so was Libby. They had fallen asleep entwined around each other in the very act of kissing, in fact, they had been unashamedly necking since the bus left

London early that morning—desperately necking, for
hours, each apparently craving one more gulp of the
other's spittlc as though it might be his or her last.
And now unconscious, though no doubt continuing
their love-making in their dreams, they seemed tragi-
cally frozcn, like those famous mummies trapped in
eloquent, if potentially embarrassing, postures by
the eruption of Vesuvius at Pompeii. No display of
intimacy could embarrass Saul and Libby, however,
lapped round by love and sealed off from the living
world as definitively as any Paolo and Francesca or
Romeo and Juliet out of medieval lore, and so the others in the group had simply gotten used to the sight
and even more startling sounds of their grappling
bodies, difficult as such tolerance had at first proved
among those at all inclined to jealousy.

The inseparability of Saul and Libby had posed
a challenge when it came to the initial assignment
of roommates in London, and no one had worried
more about this than the young American professor
in charge of the program, who now sat directly in
front of them: Hiawatha Musing. If, across the aislc,
his colleague and co-leader, Tony Trefthven-Woooser,
was as still in repose as an insect feigning death,
Hiawatha Musing's sleep was more like the literal
last throes of some long-suffering, but unmistakably
warm-blooded, animal. His left arm jerked regularly

and involuntarily. His legs seemed to vibrate, and this could no longer be attributed to the bumpiness of the ride, since the engine of the bus had been turned off for some time. Even his eyelids twitched, though they remained tightly, even fiercely, shut.

Hiawatha, or Hi, as he was known to his family and very few close friends, presented to the casual observer a figure whose leanness and nervous energy implied a youthfulness which contradicted his thirty-two years. Upon closer observation, this impression of youth was itself contradicted by certain facts, for example, that his blond hair was growing quite thin on top, a phenomenon which was accepted and even welcomed by Hi as a fitting reflection of the struggle his life seemed to him to be. Of average height and undistinguished build, he was dressed far less ambitiously than his English counterpart, Mr. Trefthven-Woooser, Tony preferring to uphold the high sartorial standards of his native country, while Hiawatha, as it seemed, relinquished in a stereotypically American way any pretension or desire to compete at such a game, not caring at all that his wellwashed blue jeans clashed in tone—both in the sense of color and degree of formality—with his dark gray cotton shirt, so long as the clothes were soft and all the tags had been cut out. At his collar, unbound by a tie, a little triangle of well-worn but very white undershirt showed, and gave Hi an almost priestly air. And that is what he most resembled, perhaps: the young, over-taxed pastor of a parish always on the brink of revert-ing to paganism.

It was with no sense of religious sacrifice, but rather like a wrongly-accused man whose lawyers have exhausted every avenue of appeal, that Hiawatha had at last submitted himself to the penalty of this latest pedagogical task, the supervision of twelve students on a six-week course abroad. And there could be no doubt that the sentence had been forced upon him. In fact, the chairman of the English department where Hiawatha taught back in Illinois had quite bluntly reminded him that although he was well liked as a teacher, his extracurricular contributions to life at the college had amounted to very little in the three years since he had arrived, and that a refusal to take up the offer to con-duct this course would more than threaten his future at the institution. Unlike a surprising number of academ-ics even in modern times, Hiawatha needed to teach in order to keep himself fed. And so, with the additional handicap of belonging to a tenure-track system hardly less rigid than those hierarchies prevailing in the peni-tentiary, Hi found himself trapped.

There was, however, no real reason why Hiawatha should not accept, and even enjoy, his summer ser-vice, chained though he was to a heterogeneous, high-maintenance gang of hardened adolescents, most of whom still glowed slightly from the overindulgence of their senior proms. After all, it kept him away from Boston and his family, and that ought to have made him happy. Furthermore, he liked to travel, and here was an opportunity to visit one of his favorite countries, free of charge. There was even a modest stipend attached to the teaching. And to divide the work, he had the assistance of his opposite number in England, the popular Tony, who was only too willing to keep a close eye on the little band when Professor Musing was busy with administrative concerns, arguing with the concierge at The Covington or wrangling for a group discount at the Tate. Clearly, a heap of blessings rested on Hi's brow. And yet, he could not relax.

Since before the group had left Chicago, Hiawatha had been tormented by two great fears, namely, that one of the students would either be found dead—killed by a bus in the perversely inverted London traffic, or by falling, as happens in at least one Hitchcock film, over the inadequate rails on the bell tower at Westminster Cathedral—or, alternatively but equally catastrophically, pregnant. The latter fear was not altogether unfounded, given that during his first semester of full-time teaching in Illinois, three of Hi's students had gotten themselves in the family way, as became all too apparent by the spring. Of course, no one had suggested that Hi was the father of any of

these children's children, but still it did look like he
might be promulgating liberal ideas, if not actually
employing certain pedagogical techniques for creating
a harmonious classroom popularized in the irrespon-
sible sixties. Playing on these two great worries, Hi's
best friend in the English Department, a Browning
scholar in her mid-fifties named Edwina Rhodes, had
recounted numerous horror stories of young academ-
ics who had been sued by vindictive parents after the
gruesome deaths or deflowerings of their respective
offspring, on just such scholarly excursions as *English Life in Literature* presumed to be. Both the deaths
and deflowerings, as well as the subsequent poverty
of the sued professors (one had actually ended up in
a loony bin), had been described in lurid detail, and
the result was that for days after their discussion,
Hiawatha could think of little else. In the end, and
with Professor Rhodes' approval, Hi had settled upon
taking out a separate insurance policy for the duration of the course, though his personal assets at that
time amounted to little more than the premium.

But, as the reader will no doubt already have surmised, these images of unsanctioned coupling and
death were only the recent, and in fact rather superficial, sources of fear threatening Hiawatha's peace of
mind. That his was a personality addicted to anxiety
had long been taken for granted by those closest to

him, and was fast becoming a subject of teasing among
the students on this course as well. Hiawatha took all
this with a good grace, accepting it, too, as part of his
burden. A fortuneteller in Greenwich Village, whom
he had once visited in the company of his slightly
younger, equally accomplished, but in many ways
more impressive sister, Antigone, had told Hiawatha
that he had a very old soul. Having cost thirty dollars,
the information remained with him as a reminder that
there was a reason for his anxieties—that his problems, both real and imagined, and the worries they
caused, were the accumulated problems and worries of
centuries. Naturally, when Hiawatha fantasized about
his role in life, it was rather as the untroubled taker-
of-things-as-they-came. But this trip abroad made it
clearer than ever how perfectly adapted he was to the
part of nervous parent. In other words, though Hi
might secretly have preferred to imagine himself as
the young, carefree star of this international adventure—the male version of Madeline—upon arrival in
England he was forced to confront the fact that he was
really Miss Clavell.

Now, asleep in a stationary bus on a stretch of
road that unfurled like an endless streamer, bifur-
cating the beautiful, haze-blotted Camford Downs,
it was as though Hiawatha, in his dreams, had never
actually left his own country, but instead was stuck

in some dreadful unending television series set back in Illinois, a nightmare version of a situation comedy in which the college was transformed (as an unconscious indication of what Hi felt was the intellectual level of the institution) into a high school. The allegorical episode from which he was futilely trying to wake himself right now might have been described in the program guide as follows:

Ruthie turns out to be storing explosives in her locker, and Kimberly Ann disappears. Herman commits bigamy with Sarah and Mame. Saul and Libby ponder the pros and cons of home abortion, and Rupert goes on a rampage, wounding Michael and most of the other students. Meanwhile, newcomer Molly (Jennessica Passion Flapp, in her television debut) scandalizes Rattstown High when she goes out for the swim team—the BOYS' swim team, that is!

Suddenly, with a great jolt, Hiawatha was delivered from his nightmare. Mr. MacMenzies had started the engine. The coach was moving. The students were waking up, laughing and chatting, feeling that this was sufficient cause for celebration. Hiawatha stretched and looked around. Immediately behind him, Libby and Saul were active again. Hiawatha didn't mind in the least; in fact, he, too, felt an exhilaration, realizing that the course was half over, and that they would soon arrive at Lostlindens, the great country house, where it would be easier to keep an eye on all of them than it had been in London. He sat up, smiling broadly and generously, fairly sure in his mind that, so far, not one of them was pregnant or dead.

II

LADY LUCY AT HOME

(Wherein a famous relic is impugned)

Lady Lucy Elevenish leaned artfully over the *bonheur-du-jour*, careful from prior experience not to throw all of her weight upon it. She had heard the distant approach of Feathers, her butler, and this was the pose in which she habitually chose to be come upon by servants and friends alike, as though in the very act of readying herself to begin a letter. There was no writing paper anywhere in the sunny morning room where she sat, but that presented no particular inconvenience, as Lucy Elevenish had penned nothing longer than her own name since her arrival in this country, over twenty years earlier, as the young wife of Sir, at that time merely Mister, Manfred Elevenish.

Lucy was now nearly fifty, a tall woman of variegated angles who, when standing up, might fruitfully be compared to an elaborate medieval pricket reconceived by Giacometti. Over this surprisingly articulated frame it was her habit to throw a large number of very expensive fabrics—dark, figured velvets overlapping with coarsely-woven, brightly-colored stuffs. The effect she aimed at, apparently, was one of extreme chromatic and textural richness, though one of her old friends had remarked behind her narrow back that every one of Lucy's outfits reminded her of a thick sample book of flock wallpapers. In any event, she cut an impressive figure, complete with fringes, irregularly-spaced beads, and heavy, "artistic" jewelry, the entire work topped by a long and severely-coifed head which seemed almost like a reduced, summary version of the larger cubist body below.

As already noted, Lucy had been in England for twenty years now, but she had needed only a fraction of that time to purge herself of almost all traces of her Texan origins, with the exception of her Texan money, which she did not abjure. At this point, she claimed, in an accent not quite traceable to any county or province of the United Kingdom but loudly enough to be heard in several of them, that she had only ever visited "the States" once, and that as a grown woman. Perhaps she felt that this unpatriotic subterfuge had been forced upon her by her circumstances; she was, after all, the mistress of a great country seat, and that implied the upholding of great English traditions, in her zeal to succeed at which it is perhaps understandable that she re-cast her distant past. Unlike Marie Antoinette, with whom in other ways she might be said to identify, she was not going to let her foreign upbringing hinder her designs among the natives of her new home.

The country seat in question was indeed a great one. Lucy's husband, a respected scholar and reader in seventeenth-century literature at Woodbridge College, had inherited Lostlindens, the house and its extensive grounds, fifteen years earlier from a collateral relation. Sir Manfred himself belonged to the old family of Elevenishes who originally hailed from Surrey. In 1770, Sir Manfred's ancestor, Mr. Watkins Elevenish (an ale merchant who, according to descendants, had been on intimate terms with James Boswell, though he is not mentioned in any of the latter's voluminous correspondence), had married Angelica Fitzmaron, daughter of the last Earl of Bothwick, and his sole heir. The tale is often told that when, in preparation for the nuptials, Lord Bothwick of Lostlindens had paid a courtesy visit to his daughter's future in-laws, he memorably and without forethought or regard to feelings declared the Elevenish house "not near large enough to store two of ye better wigs in!" Though it is tangential to our story, it is perhaps worth noting that ever since that date, the old Elevenish estate has deferentially been known by the name "The Wigpot." It is certainly true that, by the standards of the Earl's own home in Cambridgeshire, which was effectively transferred to the Elevenish family upon his death only two years after the marriage, The Wigpot was aptly termed. Lostlindens, on the other hand, was one of the largest and most magnificent houses in England.

Now reduced to occupying the northernmost four thousand acres of the lush Camford Downs, Lostlindens was a property already famous in the sixteenth century, when the Bothwicks had received it from the Crown. If The Wigpot was baptized in a typically aristocratic and, in retrospect, amusing way, Lostlindens had received its name in somewhat less humorous circumstances. In 1543, shortly after Sir Hugh Bothwick was created the first Earl, he decided to build an imposing residence on his country estates, selecting an elevated site at the edge of a verdant linden forest, with views across the downs to Camford and, beyond that, Cambridge itself. Spending twelve years and most of his fortune on his showplace, Lord Bothwick was at last on his way to completing the project when, on the very night he set out from London to sleep in his new house for the first time, one of the worst storms in history was unleashed. The Earl's coach was actually overturned, and though he survived, his house was severely damaged. Among the effects of the storm, the beautiful linden forest was utterly devastated, not a single tree of that genus left standing. Though the house had been rebuilt and enlarged periodically over the centuries, all efforts to replant the linden forest had failed, and the memory of the former setting was perpetuated only by the nostalgic name.

The erection and subsequent partial destruction of Lostlindens provided a dramatic prologue to the house's eventful history, a history in which notable personages occasionally played a part. For example, there was an old legend, frantically debated among historians, that the young William Shakespeare had lost a boot in the park as he was hastily but indirectly making his way from a poaching charge at Charlecote to London, where he would become the most celebrated denizen of the underworld that was sixteenth-century English theater. The putative boot, really no more than a swatch of cracked leather, was preserved under glass in the great hall. More conventional visits were paid in subsequent periods by such disparate luminaries as Angelica Kauffman, Charles Dickens, Woodrow Wilson, and Lucille Ball. And throughout its long evolution, the house had repeatedly been the subject of architectural interest: for example, Horace Walpole, in the eighteenth century, mocked what he felt were the "enormous trivialities" of the new wings, whereas in the next century, Pugin praised the recent gothic refacement of those same appendages.

Even the most cursory account of Lostlindens must make sad note of the decline of the intertwined Bothwick and Elevenish families in the first half of the twentieth century. By 1960, the house was an untenantable wreck; all of the furnishings had been sold off to pay death duties and gambling debts. After the demise, in quick succession, of three inheritors of the estate, it passed at last to Manfred and Lucy Elevenish. Lucy, who had been dying to take over the property since before her marriage, now threw herself into its rescue, spending untold Texan millions on every aspect of the restoration. After securing the structure of the house, she set about replacing the contents of its nearly one hundred rooms. And as the project approached completion, she successfully undertook what would be her crowning accomplishment, the obtaining of a title for her husband and herself, in keeping with their status as caretakers of so historically significant a property. Manfred was already a well-known aristocratic scholar who had published nine books on the English Metaphysical poet, Richard Crashaw. He had often been mentioned as ripe for an Honor. Having spent considerable sums on the socializing that precedes the granting of any knighthood—for Lucy Elevenish naturally aimed higher than a paltry OBE—his impatient and ingenious wife had finally clinched the deal by starting a rumor that her husband had a fatal disease, which of course proved to have been misdiagnosed shortly after the blade tapped his shoulder. That had been nearly two years ago. Now, Lady Elevenish occupied her title as comfortably and familiarly as she did the house, as if, in fact, she had been born to both. She had, quite literally, set up barricades around her pretensions to an ancient pedigree in the form of the expensive pictures and furnishings with which she continued to overload the place.

Among the former was a plethora of portraits. Half-lengths of hawknosed magistrates and their beady-eyed wives by splashy but somehow unconvincing artists like Raeburn and Lawrence intermingled with more ostentatious full-lengths of well-born statesmen fingering their chivalric gewgaws, painted, for the most part, by Reynolds near the end of his career. A famous series of female likenesses, known collectively but posthumously as the Lostlindens Beauties, constituted eight life-size ninnies tripping off porticoes and steadying themselves against urns, their jeweled aigrettes bobbing like baby chicks for grain, the entire group fittingly and accurately eternalized by Gainsborough. The long gallery at Lostlindens was said by Lady Elevenish's waggish friends to resemble nothing so much as the backstage area of a Covent Garden gala, with all the performers lined up to use one lavatory.

In the very room where Lady Elevenish now sat not writing was the picture she preferred above all, an enormous, brightly-colored image of a florid young woman in ancient costume dancing around what looked to be a pallid, lascivious satyr. This was generally regarded as the most successful effort by the short-lived Regency artist, Mandible Smee, whose name appeared on the lower part of the heavy gilt frame, just above the title of the work, *Lady Georgiana Trill, Later Countess Sprocket of Poole, Decorating a Statue of Pan with a Garland of Harebells and Grape Fern.* To her mind, this was Lady Elevenish's greatest coup in the connoisseurial line; the picture had cost very little at auction, obliterated as the scene had been by thick layers of varnish and dirt. But the triumph of the picture, like the subject itself, had emerged only later, for, upon cleaning, it became unmistakably clear that Lady Georgiana was the exact double of Lady Lucy, and the latter had received innumerable compliments on the uncanny atavism of what were assumed to be her ancestor's features, since hanging the work prominently in the morning room where she most often received her guests.

A perfectly pitched tap at the door of this room was now followed by the entrance of Feathers, impressive embodiment of an ancient and dwindling occupation. The Elevenishes' butler, whose actual name was Mr. Featherstone, was a tall man, completely bald, with a long-suffering but intelligent face and an appropriately dignified, even funereal, voice.

"M'Lady," he began, after a momentary pause, and before another of longer duration. Apparently he felt that this dirge-like greeting should be sufficient to convey the information he had to impart.

"Yes, Feathers?" said Lady Elevenish loudly, turning on her elbows, and looking up from her imaginary correspondence.

"M'Lady," repeated Feathers, as though to allow her a second chance.

"Yes, Feathers, what is it?" She felt herself on the brink of having to become haughty.

Feathers said nothing, merely directing his inscrutable gaze deeper into his mistress's delicately rouged and powdered face. After a moment, and as though she had been physically poked by her servant, she made a little gesture with her long hands, to indicate that she suddenly remembered the business on which he had come.

"Oh yes, of course. What time is it, exactly?" She only appended the last word, "exactly", in order to draw it out, so that it sounded more like "eggsooahctly". After so many years, such phonetic creativity was second nature to her.

"Just two, M'Lady," replied Feathers, with maddening nonchalance.

"Yes, they should be here by now. Have they telephoned? I suppose I must go and see to the last minute arrangements with Cook."

"Yes, M'Lady," were Feathers's final words on the subject, to indicate which he dropped his voice definitively, producing a low sound like the last chord in a Christian hymn. Then, noiselessly, he turned to leave the room.

As Lucy watched her butler close the door, she remembered how for years she had been forced to fight a binary urge to slap and tip him at the end of each of their little encounters. She may have become, in her own mind, more English than the English, but her pace, and her consequent impatience, along with her innate distrust of discretion, were pure American.

Now she rose up, considering without enthusiasm the imminent visit of these mainly foreign strangers, fourteen of them, not counting the driver. She did not eggsooahctly regret having made the invitation; at the time, it had seemed so noble, and would provide her with a good opportunity to show off her famous and elegant house and her aristocratic way of life, something in which she had not been indulged by her adoptive countrymen to the extent she felt was her due. That this group was made up mostly of students was even more appealing, because the young are so easily impressed. Still, offering to put them up for the weekend had been excessive, and she only wished that she could blame someone other than herself for having made such a suggestion. Not that there wasn't room for them all, she considered with self-satisfaction, but she only had two maids, and they were quite grumpy and expensive enough as it was.

Well, thought Lady Elevenish, in the middle of the summer what else is there to do but entertain? And it would be more tolerable with her husband away. Somehow, Sir Manfred always managed to wedge himself in between his wife and her pleasures as hostess, as though ready at any moment to remind their guests of how the happy couple had met at The University of Texas, where, in 1974, pretty Lucille Lorimer had been a pupil in a sophomore poetry class taught by her future husband, at that time a young and ever-so-English visiting professor. Lucy had swooned when she discovered the details of his crested heritage. Manfred had found himself smitten when she confessed her love and the more tangible details of her own patrimony. They had eloped in late October. Shortly afterward, at her insistence, they had moved back to his homeland, which immediately became her own. All of which, she felt, was nobody's business but theirs.

Now Manfred was away in New Zealand, looking into some vital Crashaw papers which had turned up unexpectedly there. Manfred was often away now. To tell the truth, the married couple had not been getting along very well of late. In fact, ever since her successful handling of the knighthood affair (she had invented and disseminated the rumors of her husband's terminal illness all on her own, wanting the result, which she never doubted, to come as a surprise, which it certainly did), he had hardly looked her in the face. Lady Elevenish knew that her husband was every bit as ambitious as she was, so she assumed that these latest signs of disaffection simply denoted the next, perfectly natural stage in the progress of long-term conjugal affiliation. She had endured numerous such phases throughout their twenty-five years of marriage, consoling herself on those occasions, as now, with lengthy mental comparisons between her own life and that of her one and only girlhood idol, Consuelo Vanderbilt. That famous heiress had sacrificed love to become the Duchess of Marlborough, and if she could do it, then so could Lucille Lorimer. Of course, Lady Elevenish willfully refused to follow the Vanderbilt story to its conclusion in France, where Consuelo ended up after divorcing the Duke and relinquishing her title. Renunciation was not a word in Lucy's vocabulary; she detested the French, and besides, she had spent far too much money on Lostlindens ever to consider giving it up. If anybody must go, it must be Manfred.

With thoughts such as these, she had worked herself up into something of a bad mood by the time she reached the kitchens on the ground floor of the south wing. Fortunately her cook, a large, ribald, middle-aged woman with a grand protuberance in the center of her face that might best be described as a "double-nose," knew precisely the tonic for her mistress's distemper. And so the two of them sat down on a stainless steel bench to share a stiff concoction of Pimm's Number Two Cup, celery salt, and *crème de cassis*.

"So then, just you and the young folks and the two professor types, eh?" said Mrs. Shant, settling into her seat.

"Yes, but don't forget that Millie and Coral are also coming down," said Lady Lucy, still somewhat irritably. "I'm sure I told you, Mrs. Shant." Her cook could be so maddeningly absent-minded. But this was not Lucy's real concern at present. She was still thinking of Sir Manfred, and of how she, too, ought to have had a go as Duchess of Marlborough.

"Oh yes, don't you worry, I did 'ear you say et the first time. And I've cooked sufficient for an army," Mrs. Shant responded in a light and soothing tone.

"What are we going to serve them, then?" inquired Lucy, distractedly sipping her drink.

"Well, ma'am, I've just cut the 'eads off sixty quails," replied the cook, cackling softly through her oversized nostrils. "So we're starting with those. What's left of 'em, I mean. Not the 'eads, but the bodies." Mrs. Shant was a very good-natured soul who was able to see the amusing side of even the most mundane situations.

While the two women were thus engaged in an increasingly convivial conversation concerning the menu, the coach carrying *English Life in Literature* at last crunched over the gravel at the rear of the house, where, a long time ago, the lindens had been. As the students unloaded their bags from the bus, Feathers monomially alerted Lady Elevenish of their arrival. With a parting taste of the sauce for the quails, and with a considerably lighter heart than she had borne half an hour earlier, Lucy left the kitchen for the hall. There, Feathers and the two maids were already busy helping to bring in the suitcases.

When Lady Elevenish came upon them, most of the students were standing about or stretching their legs after the long ride. Sarah and Mame were talking quietly in a corner by the door, clearly impressed by the size and splendor of the great entryway, while Herman Wadkin, upon seeing the spectacular wooden staircase rising at the far end of the room, let out a loud "Wow!" before bending down to tie his shoe. Michael Teller inspected the stucco reliefs at close range, and Kimberly Ann attempted to calculate the precise center of the enormous space. Under the watchful eye of Paula Simon, Tony Trefthven-Woooser left his luggage to the butler and made his way confidently up to Lady Lucy, who was too overwhelmed at this moment to have welcomed anyone aloud. She was cordially shaking the young Englishman's hand when something horrifying caught her eye.

In between two great pier glasses, a large girl had seated herself on the carpet, right in front of the case containing the priceless article of Elizabethan footwear. The case was open, and the girl, who had removed her own shoe, was apparently trying to pull on the ancient boot, whose last wearer may well have been The Bard himself. Lady Lucy was actually, and unprecedentedly, speechless.

"Ruthie!" someone called out suddenly, in a stern voice which was, however, clearly unused to admonishment.

Lady Elevenish, hastening silently in the direction of Ruthie Slatt, looked up, and found herself face to face with the young American leader of the troupe, Hiawatha Musing. Something in the gentle, worried expression of the young teacher took her aback and immediately assuaged her anger. She actually turned and smiled at the big spotty girl, placidly removing from the latter's clutches the famous relic, which she proceeded to replace in its glass case. Then, while Ruthie muttered something about "that thing" being "no way a boot, much less Elizabethan," and all the others looked on in suspense, Lady Elevenish turned again to Hiawatha.

"Oh it's nothing," she said, her smile widening. After which, opening her arms in a large gesture, like a duchess in a Regency play, she proclaimed loudly, "Welcome."

Abruptly dropping his gaze, Hiawatha suffered a minute spasm, like a hardly perceptible chill. Years later, he would remember this little *frisson*, which was the fluttering physical expression of a momentary hesitation, a deep-seated but apparently illogical feeling of dread. Perhaps this was only embarrassment for his student's appalling behavior, or gratitude for his hostess's magnanimity in forgiving it. Or perhaps he was the victim of a purely sensory coincidence, the grand setting and simple greeting reminding him in a flash of the famous foyer scene in *Dracula*. Perhaps, most plausibly of all, he was coming down with

something. But before he had time for conscious con-
sideration, he found himself at Lady Lucy's side. The
boot, clearly a bad omen, was put behind them, and
they all made their way deeper into the house.

III

A MEMORABLE FEAST

(And several lively discussions thereat)

A FTER THE INFAMOUS INCIDENT OF RUTHIE AND THE boot, which had been so stunningly defused by Lady Elevenish, the students were all shown to their various bedrooms, the arrangements for which had been formalized in advance by Lady Elevenish's housekeeper, a very thorough and efficient woman who was currently away visiting a sick ex-husband in Cornwall. At Lostlindens, several though not all of the students were allotted single rooms; this would allow some temporary relaxation of the claustrophobia they had experienced at The Covington, and to which they would again be subject when they moved on a few days later to a dormitory at Woodbridge

College, where they would spend the last two weeks of the course. As the group made its way *en masse* up the elaborately-carved, sixteenth-century oak stairway, Tony Trefthven-Woooser inserted himself between his colleague and Lady Elevenish, explaining without explicit encouragement the origins of his family name.

"Yes, it's an ancient family. That is to say, two families. 'Trefthven' is old Welsh—we go back to pre-Saxon times. The 'Woooser' is Norman, undoubtedly from the French, 'Où, sieur?' According to family tradition, that was the question posed by my ancestor when his liege lord, William, Duke of Normandy, informed his knights that they were going to conquer England. The three consecutive 'o's came to be considered a mark of great distinction."

Lady Elevenish seemed only vaguely to be listening to the handsome young scholar, who moved swiftly from an exegesis of his name to compliments on Lostlindens, which put him in mind, so he said, of his own family's estate, Chilblains, in fact a dilapidated stone tower without electricity on the border of Wales, now in the possession of a dissolute cousin. Lady Elevenish, somewhat to her own surprise, found herself concentrating instead on the conversation taking place just behind her, between Hiawatha Musing and Ruthie Slatt. Ruthie was dragging along her heavy rucksack as though she clearly felt that, in such a setting if not always, somebody else should be carrying it for her. Hiawatha ignored the protests implicit in her sullen features, addressing her with an air of cautious conviction.

"Honestly, Ruthie, you know better than to touch, much less try on, anything in someone else's house. What if you'd damaged the boot?"

"It wasn't a boot," interrupted Ruthie, whose surliness may have been a perverse indication of her shame.

"More importantly," continued Hiawatha, in a voice that was hardly above a whisper, "it wasn't yours. I want you to speak to Lady Elevenish as soon as you've settled yourself in, and tell her you're sorry." Hiawatha might, from his tone, have been coaxing a five-year-old to at least TRY kindergarten. But it seemed to work, for Ruthie said nothing more. Kimberly Ann, not far behind, sniggered aloud.

Meanwhile, the others were chattering softly and, for the most part, enthusiastically, as they went searching for their names on little tags tacked to the doors of the bedrooms on the second floor. Rupert didn't mind it when he accidentally tripped Paula Simon. Herman, Paul, and Molly, in varying measures, worried that they might not be adjacent to one another, though it turned out that Molly had her own room right next door to the one her friends were sharing. Saul and Libby disappeared into a room that had only Libby's name on it. Thus eventually they all vanished from the long corridor, having been informed by Feathers, in what was for him an extraordinary indulgence in speech, that dinner would be served in the formal dining room at seven.

The dining room at Lostlindens—or, more accurately, the banqueting saloon—was perhaps the chief glory among the interiors of the house. It was the largest autonomous space after the hall, and whereas the latter area maintained the heavy, timbered and dark- paneled atmosphere of the Elizabethan period to which it dated, the saloon was a glorious rose and ivory celebration of the English rococo. Ivory in the literal sense, for there were carved panels of that material set in the borders around the enormous doors at either of the room's shorter ends. One of the largest Aubusson rugs in private hands covered the parquet floor, and the richly-stuccoed rectangular ceiling was transformed into three glittering oval galaxies by enormous chandeliers copied from those in the grandest of George IV's reception rooms at Buckingham Palace.

When the students trickled in to take their places around the many-leaved mahogany table, they found themselves overwhelmed by the splendor of the setting. Herman Wadkin actually tiptoed to an empty chair, like a bear in a ballet. The table was lavishly set with Lady Elevenish's "everyday" china, a Coalport service decorated with scenes from the Grand Tour. The silverware reflected the crystal, the crystal refracted the figures seated before it, each of whom touched it reverentially as though to prove that it was real. And in the center of the table, like an octopus rising up through the pale blue linen cloth and the anemones clustered around it, a spectacular Paul Storr epergne uncoiled its many arms, each one ending in a little heap of molded chocolates, marzipan, and *marrons glacés*.

Though the seating had not been prearranged, Lady Elevenish continued to illustrate her gracious manners by greeting personally each member of the group as they came down, and directing them to the table. She placed Tony Trefthven-Woooser at the opposite end from herself, which flattered him, though that was not her primary aim in doing so. On either side of Tony, she seated one of her own more recently-arrived friends: Millie Dumont, a rich American woman with wiry gray hair and a musical laugh, and Coral Marsden, another American who had lived in this country for some time, a tall, horsey blonde whom Lady Elevenish was training to become pure English like herself. The rest of the group, Lady Elevenish allowed to seat themselves, with the exception of Hiawatha, whom she placed directly beside her, causing him a certain amount of apprehension as to the adequacy of his conversational skills in such an august presence.

At precisely seven, when the chimes of numerous clocks sounded and resounded throughout the house, Feathers entered the room, followed by the two maids and a teenage boy. As they began to serve the melon soup, Hiawatha automatically performed a head count, which was interrupted by a familiar voice behind him.

"What's all this?" said Ruthie Slatt, with a suspicious snarl. She had come down a few minutes late, and this was undoubtedly her way of expressing awe at the vastness of the dining room and the richness of its contents. Ruthie had apparently just taken a shower or bath, because her damp, inconsistently dyed hair was standing punkishly on end, like a handful of rubber bands of varying thickness and hue.

"These are called plates," said Kimberly Ann, in a voice like treacle. She had been the first to arrive at the banquet, lingering some distance from the table before at last seating herself immediately to the left of Lady Elevenish at the head. "People eat off of them." And then, when no one else seemed to hear her joke, she laughed shrilly for them all.

Hiawatha groaned inwardly while a glaring Ruthie found her seat.

Before long, a relatively pleasant conversational rhythm was established at the table; it rose and fell and rippled here and there with laughter and guffaws. Though initially daunted by the quails, the students discovered, upon tasting them, that they were delicious; the entire meal was, from a gastronomical as well as a social perspective, proceeding very smoothly, despite occasional frowns from Ruthie when she was interrupted in explaining all about her father's close ties to the Mafia back home.

"Oh yes, he's very good friends with The Family, as they call themselves in Chicago. We've often had people for dinner who later turned up dead. And my father knows exactly how much it costs to have somebody killed anywhere in the world."

Some of the students, including Paula Simon and Sarah Magister, shifted uncomfortably in their seats. Michael Teller tried, unsuccessfully, to picture himself as a hit man. Mame Freeline rolled her eyes, and Kimberly Ann continued to scowl between tiny mouthfuls of malletted venison. Others were entirely oblivious to what was going on around them, the best example of this category provided as usual by Saul and Libby, who, though not exactly sharing a single seat, nevertheless overlapped significantly below the tablecloth. Tony Trefthven-Woooser was conveniently wrapped up in charming Lady Elevenish's two American friends.

"Oh yes, Trefthven-Woooser is a name as old as England itself," he said, concluding his speech on the topic for the second time that day. Then he added, even more charmingly, "And tell me now, what are your backgrounds?"

The horsey Coral Marsden, to avoid inquiry into her own origins—her father had been a rag-rug wholesaler in West Virginia, before his daughter had married money—answered proudly for her friend.

"Oh Millie's got a very interesting name. Her first name, that is!"

"Millie? That stands for Millicent, doesn't it?" asked Tony, with great simplicity.

"Not in her case," continued Coral, suddenly very grave. "'Millie' is short for 'Mille Fiori', the Venetian glass technique. Millie's mother, an internationally renowned hostess, was equally famous as a collector of paperweights."

Throughout this interchange, as throughout most of the meal, Millie herself smiled merrily but said nothing, putting down her wine glass only long enough to have it refilled. It was a running joke among their set that coasters were wasted on Millie.

At the opposite end of the table, Hiawatha studied Lady Elevenish while Kimberly Ann regaled her with a sweeping, and far from concise, history of the superior state of Maryland. In the midst of which, Lady Elevenish turned abruptly away to talk to her other partner, leaving Kimberly Ann to the impossible task of seducing Rupert Augustus with tales of ante-bellum magnificence. Hiawatha now had the undivided attention, not to say scrutiny, of his hostess. He squirmed slightly beneath her avid gaze.

Hiawatha had actually encountered Lucy Elevenish once before. Two years earlier, she had been seated next to him at a dinner at Clare College in Massachusetts, where Hi's sister, Antigone, taught chemistry, and where Hi had come to give a lecture in a poetry symposium in which Lucy's husband was also a speaker. Having quickly exhausted his fund of compliments on her house, Hiawatha now reminded her of that former meeting.

"Aooh of cawse! I thoat you seemed owfully familiar!"

This odd way of speaking would have puzzled Hiawatha, had he not distinctly recalled hearing from another guest at that earlier dinner that Lucy Elevenish was a Texan in denial.

"I say!" Lady Elevenish continued in a loud but interested tone, "Didn't your sister wind up marrying that poor professor? The one whose wife was buried under his owld house?"

Hi was happy to give his hostess a summary version of that mystery, in which he and his sister had played so large a part, the details of which are recorded elsewhere.

"And now she and Cornelius are married, and she's expecting a kid," Hiawatha said, a little wistfully, bringing his story to an end.

Lady Elevenish paused before responding.

"We never hawd any children, Mahnfred and I. A great pity, I suppose."

In making these veiled emotional declarations, Lady Elevenish was acting somewhat out of character, though Hiawatha could not be expected to know this, having met her only once before. After another pause, which Hi found it difficult to know how to fill, she went on, more brightly.

"Dew you like children?"

Hiawatha did like children; in fact, he was extremely fond of them. But other people's. And to be honest, his fondness was more usually pity than affection. It was parents Hiawatha didn't like. About them, about parenting in general, Hi had no illusions. In fact, on a recent lightning visit to Debenhams Department Store in London, Hi had been reminded by a woman's repeated twisting of her little boy's arm of the basic injustice inherent in all parenting. And of course it was worse in his own country, where regularly, in shopping centers and parking lots, he was forced to witness parents making a public show of abusing their offspring. No, in Hi's mind, parents were, generally speaking, the most terrible thing the so-called civilized human race had produced thus far. The great exception, of course, being his own mother.

"Oh I like them well enough," he said at last, disinclined to express himself fully on the topic to a relative stranger. But then he decided to risk an addendum.

"It's what people do to them that I don't like."

"I know what you mean," replied Lucy Elevenish, leaning forward as though expecting to hear a detailed account of the young professor's own childhood sufferings. Whether or not Hi was aware of the particular nature of her curiosity would be difficult to say. Nevertheless, he leaned forward, too.

"You know," he began, in that soft tone so unusual for an American, which Lady Elevenish found strangely compelling and even attractive, "about what happened earlier, with Ruthie and the relic . . ." Here, Hiawatha glanced toward the rambunctious student and smiled, as a way of dissembling the actual topic under discussion. But there was no need, as Miss Slatt was at that moment fully engaged in extorting from Michael Teller a show of interest in her father's criminal connections.

"I mean, I have to say I admired your patience, and I thank you for it."

Lady Elevenish stared at Hiawatha, as if she suspected, and even hoped, he might be teasing her. She was unused to being appreciated, especially for patience. Then, when she realized he was serious, she tossed her tinted hair and said rather loudly,

"Oh awnestly, that's awl forgawtten. In fact, I'll tell you a little secret." Here she lowered her voice to an intimate rasp, which was also noticeably more American. "Three or four years ago, Manfred and I had someone in from The Victoria and Albert Museum—a scrawny little man with bad breath and an orange beard—and this expert, as they claimed he was, said that the leather in that old case only dated from the 1860's. That's right! It's more likely to be Abraham Lincoln's boot than William Shakespeare's. Of course we made a nice donation to the V&A, with the understanding that the visit was inconclusive. After all, it's the main reason you American tourists come to see the place when it's open to the public in May."

Hiawatha listened with fascination to this confession, slicing a peach and then carefully sipping his wine. "Well still, whose ever shoe it turns out not to be, I'm sorry that it happened. And if Ruthie hasn't yet come to you and apologized herself"—here he was going to say 'she will,' but changed his mind and sentence—"count your blessings."

"Oh but it was you who handled her so well," said Lucy graciously. "I heard you call her, and I felt, all of a sudden, that my anger was unnecessary. Your calm obviated my storm."

Hiawatha, who could never think of himself as calm, was again puzzled and, a little arrogantly perhaps, surprised by Lady Elevenish's vocabulary, and even more by her apparent desire and ability to please, which was not at all what he remembered about her from his earlier encounter. What he recalled was a woman who insisted—unwisely, given the frequent absurdity of her pronunciations—on being heard by everyone in the room. Now here she was, practically whispering confidences to him. Furthermore, he couldn't help but notice that her American accent was coming back, as her British fell away.

For her part, Lady Elevenish was struck by something indefinable in the young American professor, with whom she had as yet exchanged hardly more than fifty words. Physically, Hiawatha seemed to her almost negligible, or at least insubstantial, and yet she sensed a largeness of spirit and a warmth in his proximity that was a balm to her chilly soul. Somehow he represented for her at that moment—it is not too much to say, at that juncture in her career—a world in which all her money and her artificial ancestry counted neither for her, nor against. Though Hiawatha was not from Texas but Massachusetts, still it was as if, when he spoke, Lady Elevenish heard a tinkling bell that called her back to another place, and to a time that predated even her anglophilia, after all the driving force of her adult life. In a word, Hi made the middle-aged woman homesick for a home she could no longer claim, and she suddenly found herself ardently wishing that all the other people in the room would disappear, so that she could be alone with him, sitting on a bench in the garden, telling him the innumerable pent-up truths of her life, before she forgot them once and for all.

As a way of at least prolonging their conversation, she summoned Feathers and directed him to bring in some after-dinner drinks, something she had not originally planned to do. If Hiawatha had been a more commanding person, or more at his ease, he might have tried to discourage her, fearing as he did that the students would become drunk and do things that would make the boot incident seem like a mild burp. For instance, in her constant bid for more attention than Ruthie, Kimberly Ann might break into Lady Elevenish's boudoir and start trying on her clothes. And he dreaded to think what Libby and Saul might do if, under the influence, they were to shuck their meager store of inhibitions. So he excused himself for a moment and went to have a word with his co-leader. Leaning against the latter's chair, Hi whispered his assessment of the situation. Tony, feeling by now a tiny bit slighted by the distance between their hostess and himself, took it out on Hi.

"Well it's not as though they'll be driving," said Trefthven-Woooser irritably and rather too audibly, running his hand through his silvery mane. "This is England, after all. If Lady Elevenish wants to regale us, it wouldn't be polite to decline."

Thus dismissed, Hiawatha returned to his seat, with Tony looking enviously on. When he was back at his place beside Lady Elevenish, Hi thanked her for the *Baume de Venise*, with which she was filling his smallest glass, and then told her that he thought the students shouldn't be given too much liquor or they might tear her house down.

"Oh what does it matter?" laughed Lady Elevenish, licking a drop of the sweet muscat from her wrist. The gesture struck Hi as being flagrant—but flagrantly what? Perhaps just flagrant. He wasn't given too much time to speculate on the trajectory of Lucy's mood, because before long she was questioning him again.

"Tell me, have you always wanted to teach? I mean, is that your true calling?"

Perhaps because they had all been drinking, this question, posed ingenuously enough, struck Hi as being terribly important. In fact, it glanced a tender nerve, and what with the tension he had been living with since the course began—and no doubt longer than that—it seemed vital that he make himself clear in answering.

"Well, I can't say it's the end of all my plans. I would like to do a lot of other things besides teaching. I mean, I love my work and all, but sometimes I wonder what that work really is. In my country," Hi made this explicit distinction between his and his hostess's native lands, almost as a way of thanking her for her interest in him, and for her kindness to them all. "In my country, teaching has become such a lowly occupation, looked down upon, ill-paid. What people respect us for, the imparting of information, is more reliably relegated to computers. What they should respect us for, namely, the individuality of our visions and our ways of expressing ideas, has come to be seen as an obstacle to progress. Some days I'd rather be a lion tamer than a teacher. Some days, in fact, I think I am a lion tamer. Or at least, I try."

Lady Elevenish looked more than a little startled by this impassioned response to her somewhat disinterested, if not actually lazy, question. She could easily picture her husband grunting loudly at Hiawatha's

earnestness, if that's what this was. But then, Manfred
was one of those scholars, far from rare, who pity and
loathe all the poor people working in anything outside of their own particular spheres. For him, Richard
Crashaw was not only a "good topic" for intellectual investigation, he was also the answer to all the
questions, the riddle and its one correct response,
in terms of which Shakespeare ("Shoeless Will," as
Sir Manfred familiarly referred to him) was merely
a most promising precursor, and Robert Browning,
whom Lady Elevenish vaguely recalled was the topic
of Hiawatha's own research, justifiable only to the
extent that he referred to or emulated or could be
shown to be conscious of the earlier writer.

Having identified himself as a lion tamer,
Hiawatha for his part immediately blushed and bit
his lip, angry at himself for being at once so pompous and so trite. But Lady Elevenish, in her present, Manfred-less state, and after drinking fairly
steadily for the past three or four hours, felt herself
increasingly affected by this young man. In truth it
was more the young man than what he was saying,
since, despite looks of intense concentration that
lasted longer than was required for politeness, she
wasn't following him all that closely. Instead she
was pondering the odd notion, illustrating itself for
her now, that it often takes an interruption of our

routines to show us the true nature of our actions and, by extension, who or what we really are. In other words, thought Lady Elevenish, and more to the point, just as it is not always in the midst of falling on our faces that our clumsiness is brought most painfully home to us, but later, reflecting on or being reminded of the fall, so too it is not necessarily in the absence of many people, but in the presence of a single individual, that we recognize the specificity of our loneliness. She was not sure that this was a momentous revelation, she even had the sense to suspect that it had something to do with her earlier resentful feelings about Sir Manfred and the basic tedium of her highly successful and enviable life. But here it was before her, the mirror, in the person of a young professor with the laughably inappropriate name of a legendary Indian chief. She brought her right hand down gently onto his left wrist, which Hiawatha chose to interpret as an indication that he should elaborate or at least clarify his views on the matter of his vocation.

"What I mean is, teaching isn't everything to me. That is, I hope some day to be more than I am. That is my plan, but I admit it's rather blurry."

"Oh my dear," said the former Lucille Lorimer, and her accent was now that of a radio commentator at a rodeo—in other words, a quintessentially

Texan drawl—though her tone was rather sad, "you shouldn't ever make plans. It's as if the devil just waits for you to make plans, or to hope, and then he knows right where to get you."

So now the devil joined them in the historic dining hall. From the long fingers around his wrist, Hiawatha looked slowly up through a gathering alcohol-induced haze. The face that met his was a handsome if not a youthful one, crisply featured and well attended to. Hi hoped that his hostess wasn't going to undermine this impression of control by becoming lugubrious. In his experience, conversations that began with white wine and talk of children invariably ended in liqueur and tears, with or without confessions and one or more reds in between. His apprehension was diverted, however, when Kimberly Ann Crestview, finally sufficiently fed up with being ignored by the mistress of the house (after all, her father had paid six and a half thousand dollars to send his daughter abroad on this course, not counting the airfare), exclaimed, in a tone clearly intended to command everyone's attention,

"But Lady Elevenish, if you're serving after-dinner drinks, shouldn't the women retire to another room, and leave the men to whatever it is men talk about?"

Lady Elevenish, whose own English was so various, now looked at Kimberly Ann as though she had squealed out something in Mandarin. She couldn't think what the silly girl, all gotten up in green polyester ruffles that trailed across her bosom like Louisiana moss, was talking about. For an awkward moment, Lucy Elevenish was neither American nor English, but lost in space. Then she came back to her senses.

"Oh, here at Lostlindens, we never do such old-fashioned things." And she laughed quite openly but not unkindly. She had no intention of leaving the men alone at this particular moment. But Kimberly Ann wasn't about to let the issue end there.

"Oh, but it would be so fun," she said, gleefully clapping her hands as if she were the Queen of the Amazons summoning her maidens to a conga line. She for one wanted to see more of the house. "It would be wonderful, like in all those Merchant-Ivory films. Oh say we can!"

Due to the commanding voice in which Kimberly Ann had made her suggestion, the other students had curtailed their own conversations, and were waiting to see whether or not the women would indeed adjourn to another place, a question concerning which most of them felt no inclination whatsoever. Lady Elevenish was on the brink of producing a second, more peremptory and dismissive laugh, when Ruthie Slatt spoke up, her comment clearly directed to Kimberly Ann.

"And you wonder why you're still a virgin."

Kimberly Ann went positively mauve with rage. Some of the others laughed quietly. Tony looked at Hiawatha and shrugged, as if the students, being Americans, were suddenly outside of his jurisdiction. Before even Hi could make an attempt to tone things down, Ruthie stood up.

"And another thing," she said, like a military leader listing the shortcomings of his battalion, "where is Mr. MacMenzies?"

Lady Elevenish was happy to field this comparatively simple question.

"Why, he's eating in the kitchen, with the servants!" She was very proud of how well her servants were looked after.

"That's horrible," exclaimed a disgruntled Ruthie. "He should be here with us. It's wrong to divide people up according to class. It's unfair."

Squinting like a judge at an incompetent jury, she added emphatically,

"It's not natural!"

Kimberly Ann, lying in wait, responded with painfully precise diction, savoring every syllable.

"It's not natural for a pig to mate with a dog, but clearly it's possible."

Ruthie, stationed three seats away from Kimberly Ann, lunged sideways toward her. The epergne shook like a tree in an autumn storm, dropping some of the sweets from its branches. Hiawatha was up in a flash, pulling Ruthie off a rigid Rupert Augustus's lap, where she had landed just short of Kimberly Ann. Tony, too, sprang up, in order to restrain the latter, who was pulling Ruthie's hair. Several of the other students rose; some were a bit frightened by this turn of events, but most were tempted to howl with laughter. Millie Fiori Dumont did laugh out loud, and Coral Marsden's jaw dropped a considerable distance—she had, coincidentally, been practicing expressions of mute aristocratic astonishment for the past month. In seconds the two archenemies were on their feet, being escorted out of the room by Tony and Hi. Thankfully nothing was broken in the tumult. Lady Elevenish, resuming her best British accent, stood up.

"Well perhops we hawd better cawl it a night," she said, smiling archly in spite of herself.

At this signal that the evening was over, the students all rose to leave. One by one they approached their hostess, each making a face which indicated his or her own attitude to the recent outburst—whether of sheepish delight or embarrassment or commiseration—before saying good night and departing. In the middle of this exodus, Hiawatha returned, to apologize briefly for the second time that day.

"I'm so sorry, Lady Elevenish" he said. "Tony and I are going to talk to them right now. Sorry."

"Oh it's nothing," said Lady Elevenish, also for the second time that day. And resting her jeweled hand on his shoulder, she added, "I'll come and find you when you've straightened everything out. And please, please call me Lucy."

IV

THE WEE HOURS

*(During which many people
and things are transposed)*

WHEN MOONLIGHT RENDERED IT VISIBLE, THE
nighttime silhouette of Lostlindens was even
more impressive than that which the great house's
steep gables and crenellations presented during the
day. As luck would have it, the moon was quite large
on this particular night, weaving its way skillfully
between grey clouds like an experienced barmaid
crossing a beer hall crowded with sprawling drunks.
An owl cried out from a chink in the attic sheathing,
wishfully announcing its dominion over the glowing
dark. A fox sped after a rabbit, which disappeared
into a hole. Entire races of midges, hanging like puffs
of black soot in the air, were devoured by low-flying

bats. And the first cricket of summer sang in the little stone temple to Ceres which marked the halfway point on the path from the house to the medieval parish church with the Bothwick family burial chamber below.

Inside the great residence, every variety of postprandial charade was acted out. Mrs. Shant, for example, was still washing up after the feast, an activity which would have taken far less time but for the fact that she stopped every few minutes for a swallow of one of her famous concoctions. By eleven the goodnatured woman had fallen asleep standing up at the sink, her rubber gloves submerged in foamless grey water, snoring contentedly though her nasal megaphones. The two maids, Maggie and Dither, short for Ditherine, laughed at the sight, as they always did, on their way to their beds in the servants' wing. Feathers passed them in the hall on his own way to putting out the lights in the major rooms of the house, and said to them not so much as good night.

At roughly eleven thirty, a small window on the second story was broken by a stone, but nobody noticed.

In her own room, Molly Version paced over the Persian carpet, propelled forward and back by frustration. She had not enrolled at college in order to spend her evenings alone. As a matter of fact, her sole motivation

for matriculating had been the same as that of many
of her friends, namely, to have fun. Since her fifteenth
birthday, Molly had recognized that her definition of
fun was inherently, not to say exclusively, a sexual
one. And yet here it was, already three weeks into the
program, and she had not yet extracted more than a
vague promise from Paul Stripling that they would "do
something" when they got to the "big house." The way
Paul put it made it sound like they were going to start
their own company in jail. Why did he have to be so
shy? she wondered, pausing in her yo-yo promenade
to light a third cigarette. And if he wasn't interested,
why couldn't he just say so, and leave her and Herman to explore separate possibilities? She would have
gone straight for Herman in the first place, except that
Paul, slimmer and more malleable and obviously less
experienced, was more her type. Furthermore, she
was forced to admit, Herman seemed less keen than
football players are programmed to be. And if he was
clearly not particularly intelligent (oh, but she could
work with that), he was probably one of those selfish,
narcissistic sports stars who favored one-night stands,
and she wanted something that would last at least
until the end of the course.

   When Molly heard the little porcelain clock,
which she had taken from the nightstand by her single bed and moved into the closet to avoid its ticks

and chimes, strike a muffled midnight, she stubbed her cigarette out on the windowsill, kicked it under the rug, and strode courageously through the door in order to pay a call on her dilatory prey. Before knocking, she cast an envious glance across the corridor toward Libby's doorway, but her envy was, literally speaking, misplaced. For Libby's room, which ought technically to have contained at least Libby herself, and, less officially, both Libby and Saul, was in fact completely empty. Saul's room, on the other hand, was not empty, but this was not due to the presence of Libby or Saul. While the room assigned to Michael Teller and Rupert Augustus was, like Molly's, now curiously void of occupants. Finally, Tony Trefthven-Woooser was not doing his late-night reading in his own bed, so that he was not aware of any intrusion when, around one-fifteen am, the door of his room opened and closed quickly, its hinges creaking, but tactfully. At almost the same moment, footsteps crunched on the gravel outside the house. A light was furtively turned on in the library. Molly let out a loud and not overly satisfied giggle, before at last reemerging into the empty corridor just before two.

Mysterious, indeed, are the movements of the tribe.

But not everyone in the tribe moved so mysteriously. Sarah and Mame, after all, remained as posted, playing children's card games across Mame's bed, and laughing deliriously at frequent references to the face of Kimberly Ann when Ruthie had called her a virgin. And at the way Tony had sweated in his struggle to free Ruthie's hair. And at the very notion of "Hearts" and "Old Maid." Like older versions of Sarah and Mame, Coral Marsden and Millie Dumont were laughing over the same images in the luxurious suite they shared in a distant wing of the house. Meanwhile, hard as it may be to believe, the subjects of all this merriment, Ruthie and Kimberly Ann, were slumbering soundlessly, the latter having actually given up her single room to the former as a conciliatory gesture during their latest peace negotiations under the supervision of the two course leaders.

There was one other person who was exactly where she was supposed to be, and that was Lady Elevenish. But she was not alone. Hiawatha, at the end of a trail of his clothes, lay naked beside her on the bed, sleeping deeply and dreamlessly and more peacefully than he had in at least a month since this adventure began.

V

THE HARSH LIGHT OF DAY

(And harsher revelations made thereby)

At nine o'clock the next morning, Sarah and Mame returned to the dining room, refreshed after an evening of hilarity and sleep. They were the first to arrive, and were suitably impressed by the extensive breakfast buffet which covered the eleven-foot-long, elaborately-carved, Georgian mahogany sideboard. There were numerous Sheffield warming dishes set above little burners with live flames; these contained sausages and sundry more easily identified meats, eggs in various stages of frying, beans, tomatoes, and other traditional English matutinal favorites. In the center of the sideboard, a gigantic urn boiled water for tea, and silver toast racks punctuated the otherwise run-on sequence of tastier dishes lined up before it. Mame didn't know where to begin, so she followed her friend's lead, dropping a tea bag into a cup of boiling water and sitting down at the table to wait for some of the others to appear.

"Don't you think I should film the display, before the rest come down and destroy its symmetry?" Mame asked Sarah, reaching below her seat for her video camera.

"Well, you already recorded the dinner table. If you keep filming food, our parents will think we did nothing but eat the whole time we were here." Sarah was so good at foreseeing the way things would look to others long after they had occurred.

"Well if we're not going to film it, I think we should start taking it apart," commented Mame, who was famished. And with that, she picked up her plate and walked boldly back to the lavish spread, where she began opening the lids of the chafing dishes and selecting small portions of everything that looked good. Sarah was right behind her. As they were reseating themselves, Paul and Herman appeared. They forwent the preliminary show of tea-taking patience, immediately grabbing two plates and piling them high with food. Other than the sound of their cutlery against the dishes, they were silent. As were Rupert and Michael, when they arrived and repeated the performance of their predecessors a few minutes later.

The next person to reach the saloon was Paula Simon. She looked rather haggard, as though she had slept neither well nor long. Sarah and Mame both noted this, sympathetically interpreting it as another piece of evidence to support the theory that she was pining unhealthily for Tony Trefthven-Woooser. Paula seemed in fact not to have removed her make-up from the previous evening, so that her features seemed a bit lopsided, as if her lipstick and blush had migrated ever so slightly around her face during the night. Paula was indeed so nervous about being late for breakfast that she had neglected her characteristically brief and perfunctory *toilette*. When Rupert asked her to pass the orange marmalade, she did so with something of a grunt, and then went back to coddling her tea.

When Molly Version arrived, she took her plate of food and sat between Rupert and Mame, which caused Mame and Sarah to exchange looks of bewilderment. This was the first time that either woman could recall Molly separating herself from Herman and Paul. There was little time to speculate on this development, however, because immediately after Molly had seated herself, Hi and Tony walked in, followed closely by Lady Elevenish and her two American friends. Whereas everyone else in the room was fully dressed, Lady Elevenish wore a long, multi-colored robe of quilted Liberty fabric, tied around her waist with a crimson cord.

"Well, good morning everyone," she said upon entering. "I see you've found the food."

She appeared in high spirits, her accent hardly perceptible, as though she had forgotten to put it on, or at least tighten it, when she rose from her bed.

"Good morning," replied two or three individuals, including Herman and Coral Marsden. Most of the company were still rather sleepy. Saul and Libby, when at last they arrived, looked even more tired than Paula Simon, leading Lady Elevenish to consider admiringly how the young are capable of staying awake forever if they are in love. Neither of them so much as started when Hiawatha, rubbing his throat, suddenly sneezed, dipping his head below the table which caused the sound to reverberate like a cataract.

"God bless you!" said Lady Elevenish, who had kept her eyes on him since they had entered the room together. "Goodness, what a manly sneeze!"

Hiawatha, sitting upright again, blushed profusely, perhaps from the commotion he had caused, perhaps from the comment it had elicited.

"Sorry," he said meekly.

"I hope you're not coming down with something," continued Lady Elevenish, secretly hoping that he was, and that consequently he would not be able to participate in the field trip the class was scheduled to make to Camford. She happily pictured a whole day of nursing him at home.

"Oh no, it's nothing," replied Hi, politely, though in fact he was already certain that he had somehow caught a cold. His throat stung, and he felt an over-whelming fatigue.

While conversations around the table increased in number and volume, Hiawatha examined through gold-rimmed glasses the agenda for the day. The group was due at the Camford Museum by eleven, when they would be met by the curator of the Rutland-Gore Collection of English Narrative Pictures. Hiawatha was particularly looking forward to inspecting at firsthand the Hogarth series, *The Whore's Descent.* Still, in the midst of contemplating this prospect, a terrible thought dawned upon him. Neither Ruthie nor Kimberly Ann had yet appeared in the dining room. And while Ruthie was notoriously late, almost as a projection of principle, Kimberly Ann was just as notoriously punctual, often criticizing aloud the more casual members of the group.

"Has anybody seen Ruthie or Kimberly Ann?" asked Hiawatha, already somewhat hoarsely. And as soon as he had made the inquiry, he realized that people might think he was being facetious, especially after the events of the previous night. Sure enough, several students responded in jest.

"Whenever I see them, I head for the nearest door," said Herman laughing.

"I never look at them, so I never see them," said Paul, mimicking his friend's tone.

Hiawatha frowned. They were all aware that the absence of both young women boded ill for another day of conflict. Perhaps even now they were locked in battle, like Polynieces and Eteocles, each driving a spear through the other's bosom, or gnawing hungrily on each other's toes. When Tony rose and offered to go and get them, Paula spoke despondently.

"Well Ruthie was still asleep when I came down," she said, clearly hoping, as Sarah and Mame easily saw, to hold Tony's attention, if only for a moment.

"But you mean Kimberly Ann, don't you?" asked Hiawatha. The soreness in his throat seemed to worsen with each word he spoke.

Paula looked puzzled, then she flushed.

"What do you mean?" she asked. "Ruthie and I were roommates."

"Yes, but Ruthie and Kimberly Ann switched rooms last night. Kimberly Ann very kindly offered to give up her single as a goodwill gesture after their. . ." here Tony paused in his explanation of the effects of the reconciliation the previous evening. "After their little episode," he finished at last, without looking directly at Paula. The latter flushed again.

"No one told me," she said even more dejectedly, after another pause.

"Well I'll go and get them."

This valiant proposal came from Molly Version, who seemed happy to have an excuse to leave the room. Indeed she fairly skipped out the door, which drew upon her the tacit censure of Feathers, who had silently stationed himself there at some point during the past half hour. When Molly was gone, Hiawatha continued to ponder the odd information that Paula had given them, namely, that Ruthie was still in bed. Had Ruthie after all, and after the rest of them—with the apparent exception of Paula—had retired for the evening, decided to reject Kimberly Ann's offer of the single? Maybe there was a big spider in the latter's room. Or maybe the roof leaked.

After three or four minutes had passed, Molly returned, her gait dramatically different from that with which she had made her exit. She stopped in the doorway, blanched and quaking.

"I think there's something wrong with Ruthie," she said in a trembling voice, without coming into the room.

She's pregnant, thought Hi automatically. And then on second thought, Oh, but she *couldn't* be.

"What on earth do you mean?" said Lady Elevenish, who recognized in Molly's tone more than a hint of calamity, but found this turn of events a nuisance, preoccupied as she was with thoughts of running a hot bath for Hiawatha.

"You'd better come and see," responded Molly.

Hiawatha was conscious of a growing sense of panic, but was able to suppress it sufficiently to take charge.

"Oh all right," he spoke with feigned irritation, when in truth he was feeling dizzy and increasingly anxious. "Tony, if you wouldn't mind going to find Kimberly Ann, I'll go back with Molly to see what the matter is." Then, turning hopefully to the latter, "Did she at least respond to you?"

At this, Molly burst into tears.

"No. She didn't respond! She didn't even move! I think she's dead!"

Hiawatha hastened from the table in the direction of the hall, filled with dread, impelled against his inclinations, and not so much by curiosity as by obvious necessity. Behind him, nearly all the students had risen with a communal gasp; several, including Saul and Herman, raced out behind their teacher, in direct contradiction of Tony Trefthven-Woooser's explicit command that everyone remain where they were. Tony himself followed Hiawatha to the second floor, with Lady Elevenish, billowing in her rich gown, gathering momentum in his wake. When she and the rest of the group arrived at the open door of Ruthie's room, with Kimberly Ann's name tag still affixed to it, Hiawatha had already gone in.

Upon entering, Hi was immediately overwhelmed by a sensation of airlessness, as though the entire scene that greeted him was an arrangement of carefully preserved flowers or an elaborate composition of sea shells and stuffed birds, the whole under a bell jar, the life-size version of a Victorian diorama or taxidermy display. Once inside, Hi's own human capacity for making noise was removed from him; his shoes were quiet on the carpet, even the words he thought he was speaking aloud evaporated as they formed, and he was initially forced to accept the absolute soundlessness of the atmosphere into which he was effectively swallowed up.

Light crept round the edges of the curtains drawn over the two vertical windows and oozed in a slow cascade over the sills. With Tony now directly behind him, and the others, including Lady Elevenish, hovering silently just outside the door, Hiawatha approached the bed, in which the perfectly still silhouette of a female body was discernible.

"Ruthie!" Hiawatha cried out, almost angrily.

Ruthie didn't respond.

Lady Elevenish, reaching a hand into the room, flicked a switch, and they were all confronted suddenly, as in the glare of a lightning flash, with a revelation that Hiawatha was subconsciously but futilely trying to put off. There on the bed, tilted to one side, frozen stiff, her mouth gaping, her eyes wide as though she recognized them all, lay Ruthie Slatt. Dead. Beyond question, even for those who had never seen death before.

Hiawatha reeled backward; it was only Tony, immobilized behind him, that prevented him from falling down. Lady Elevenish was instantly by his side.

"Look, I'm going to call a doctor," she said, rising as at every crisis, though up to now most of her crises had involved no more than missing jewelry or minor rows with her husband or the servants. Hiawatha and Tony turned with her to usher the students away from the room. The latter were, without exception, visibly in shock, and several were already in tears. Molly was once again flanked by Herman and Paul, who were trying to calm her as they moved like a single creature back down the corridor. Sarah and Mame wept quietly and held hands, while Saul embraced Libby more tightly than even he had formerly thought possible. Feathers himself, who, under the direction of Lady Elevenish, was now conducting the group to a large drawing room where they would be able to collect themselves, was doing his best with limited experience to express consolation to the young people.

"Everything will be fine," he repeated softly, his face chalky white above his black lapels, his hands trembling slightly.

Hiawatha and Tony were with Lady Elevenish in her bedroom, calling the local physician, after which she dialed the number of the police. While she was talking, Hiawatha murmured to Tony something which had just reentered his mind.

"And where is Kimberly Ann?"

A mixture of fear and suspicion entered the minds of the two instructors. But they were not left to wonder for long. For even as Lady Elevenish summoned the local constabulary, a piercing scream reached them from the corridor.

"That's Paula," said Tony, as he and Hi raced out of the room in the direction of the terrible sound. Seconds later they were in the doorway of the bedroom that Paula Simon had shared, not with Ruthie, but with Kimberly Ann. And only then did the true scale of the catastrophe make itself clear.

Just inside the room sat Paula Simon in a quivering heap on the rug, with her back to the door. The curtains were open, revealing a small pane of broken glass in one corner of the large window. The two beds were spotlit by the morning sun, the nearer one neatly made up. On the far bed, the blankets had apparently been pulled off, rather messily and perhaps violently. And there against the expensive linen sheets lay the physical remains of Kimberly Ann Crestview, in a pink chiffon nightgown and matching robe, her thick hair streaming back over the pillow and the edge of the bed. Unlike Ruthie, her eyes were thankfully closed, but there was again no question of her being alive. A thin line of dried blood circled her throat, and there was blood on her mouth as well. Worst of all, lying on her back, her body seemed broken in the middle, or at least twisted in a pose that reminded Hi of the painful contortions of the fish at the end of the twine, as it is reeled in by the fisherman. Her hands were folded across her chest, and in them she clasped what was clearly the most bizarre detail of the gruesome scene, a hand-mirror, the reflective surface resting against her rigid body.

For a few seconds that seemed endless, no one said a word. Then at last Paula turned, crying, to the two instructors.

"I thought it was Ruthie," she wailed. "I thought she was still asleep! Then I came back and pulled the covers down!!"

Paula dissolved in inarticulate sobs. Tony dropped down beside her and rubbed her shoulders with his hands, by way of encouraging her to rise. She buried her face in his cashmere sweater.

Hiawatha, paralyzed—in fact, as unable to move as the two dead women before and behind him—found his mind swimming with inexplicable notions. Tony was awfully well-dressed. Lady Elevenish was not the love of his, Hi's, life. Say what you will about Ruthie, she had a sense of humor. So, for that matter, did Kimberly Ann. Molly was too young to travel. Rupert was tall and scary. Lostlindens was not a bad house to visit, but he wouldn't want to live there.

When Lady Elevenish broke his concentration with a loud cry, putting her hand on his shoulder from behind, Hiawatha had in fact come to a decision.

First he would telephone his sister, Antigone. Then he would kill himself.

VI

TWO DOWN

*(Which summary demands no
further parenthetical elucidation)*

T HAT'S RIGHT. STRANGLED."
This bleak declaration was intoned with admirable dramatic éclat by the chief of the Camford District police. Detective Superintendent Greene was a portly man in late middle-age, who seemed consciously to be cultivating a slight physical resemblance to Winston Churchill, as that renowned politician appeared during the Second World War. Which cultivation manifested itself in a deep and emotion-filled voice and a bluff, but altogether feigned, simplicity of manner. If you had ever spoken to Mrs. Greene, however, you would have been persuaded that her husband was, on the contrary, a master of almost inhumanly complex

psychological methods for running to ground criminals and wayward family members alike. He had thick lips, bulging green eyes, and the fine grey hairs along the edges of his ears were always raised as though picking up signals.

As attentive as two schoolboys summoned to the office of their principal, Hiawatha and Tony sat in stiff-backed wing chairs, listening to this imposing figure who occupied more than half of a small sofa opposite them in Lady Elevenish's morning room. In his right hand Hiawatha clutched a growing wad of tissues, with which he occasionally blew his nose or stifled a cough or sneeze. His cold had come on with amazing alacrity, as though accelerated by the excitement of the recent double revelation. He was sure, and glad, that he sounded as sick as he felt, habituated as he was to using illness as a barrier between himself and other people, as well as an excuse for expecting gentle treatment from those members of the outside world who, for whatever reason, chose to draw near. In following this strategy he was like most sick people, whether their maladies are serious or minor, or even, for that matter, wholly imaginary.

Six hours had passed since the harrowing discoveries of the morning, with all the evidence they presented of even more horrifying events that had preceded them at less precisely named times the night before. Since then a great deal had already been accomplished. Lady Elevenish had somewhat begrudgingly turned control of her house over to the local police, who had taken brief preliminary statements from the members of her staff and all of her guests, including the American students. The bodies of Ruthie and Kimberly Ann, properly examined and photographed by an astonishingly large and efficient squadron of forensic criminologists and their subsidiaries, had been removed to the Camford morgue. The families of the two unfortunate women had been informed of the tragic news, and three distraught parents (Kimberly Ann's father, Harmon Crestview, could not be found) had immediately made arrangements for their transatlantic flights. Antigone Musing, too, was on her way to Lostlindens. Though three months pregnant, Tig had received the distinct impression from Hiawatha, when he telephoned her, that he desperately depended on her aid, though he did not come right out and ask his sister to fly over. What he did communicate, however hoarsely, in between abrupt, worried silences and loud wheezing coughs, was an indisputable sense of genuine need, so that she had, upon the encouragement of her husband, who was currently attending an academic conference in California, boarded the first flight from Boston for London, where she was scheduled to arrive late that afternoon.

Now, with the investigation fully under way, Superintendent Greene was interviewing Hiawatha and Tony for the second time, in a more leisurely, speculative, and ostensibly fact-sharing session.

"And Ruthie? How did she . . . meet her end?"

Hi looked appreciatively at Tony when the latter made this remark, admiring his colleague and the English in general for the wonderful stock of polite euphemisms they always had at hand. Hiawatha, in his present blurry, and still rather shocked, state could come up with no better synonym for "die" than the crass "kick the bucket," the shame of considering which made Hi's fever go up a notch.

"We don't know for sure yet," replied a rich, avuncular voice, which reminded Hiawatha of the actor they had recently seen performing the role of John of Gaunt in *Richard II* onstage in London. "But after spending twenty-eight years in this terrible business, my guess is that she was poisoned. Possibly a drug overdose, which raises the issue of accidental or deliberate suicide, as well as murder."

This response of Superintendent Greene's was accompanied by a look that made it clear he didn't answer questions without receiving proportionately exorbitant returns vis-à-vis pertinent information. His standard method for questioning witnesses or others involved, however tangentially and innocently,

in crimes, was to confide basic but superficial and easily discovered facts, which were then to be requited
with lengthy accounts of even the most recondite and,
more often than not, useless details, suggestions, and
personal opinions. Therefore he continued.

"How do you two think she might have died? And
why? Was there anything in her behavior to suggest
that she might have been suicidal? Was there, as far as
you know, a boyfriend, here or back home? Of course,
you've already turned over copies of the students'
medical records—that will prove a great help, I have
no doubt. But aside from the physiological factors to
be considered, what was the character of Miss Slatt?
And of Miss Crestview? What was their relation to
one another? And why don't you tell me, Mr.—I'm
sorry, Professor—Musing, what was your relationship with each of them?"

Hiawatha, hating to be called on first, and after
such a myriad of inquiries, was forced to take refuge in the cool rhetoric of the professional educator,
which was so at odds with his own more rambling
and exploratory way of speaking.

"My relationship with both of them was the same,
and can be described succinctly as the normal one
connecting any teacher and his or her students."

Hi might have been reading from a pamphlet
on college etiquette. His cold—which he had little

doubt was fast developing into pneumonia—and the Laphraoig with which Lady Elevenish had tried to soothe him at lunch, seemed to threaten the wariness of his mind. He knew that he must remain alert to what was being said, even more so to what he said, and how he said it. He was braced somewhat by the slight but instinctive antagonism he always felt for the police and their inevitably accusing ways. Still, he was careful to be polite, reminding himself once again, as though he was incapable of truly retaining the fact, that this was an investigation for murder.

"That is to say, we had a natural teacher-pupil relationship."

"Yes, yes, of course," Detective Greene said, almost chuckling, as though eager to establish a friendly atmosphere of trust and understanding among intimates. "And the two girls. Did they get along?"

It was obvious from the point to which the detective sharpened this question that he had already been apprised to some extent of the relationship existing between Ruthie and Kimberly Ann. Hiawatha now attempted to flesh out the sketch for him, in a way that would not appear colored by subjective exaggerations of what must in any case be described as the brightly-hued characters of the two deceased students.

"Ruthie Slatt was a very smart girl, but she had a temper and was very independent in her thinking. She

was loud and bossy, but I found her rather fascinating."
Here Hiawatha seized an opportunity to sneeze loudly.
"Kimberly Ann was more traditional, more genteel—I
suppose you could say she was more feminine, but her
behavior was also noticeably more artificial than Ruthie's. Kimberly Ann had a temper, too. For some reason,
which I never understood, the two of them didn't get
along at all. Tony and I discussed it on more than one
occasion, and neither of us could figure it out."

At this point, wanting to show his own eagerness
to collaborate with the authorities, Tony spoke up,
leaving Hiawatha to discreetly blow his nose.

"Yes, I myself conducted the first conflict-resolution
meeting between the two girls in London."

Inspector Greene raised his eyebrows playfully at
this relatively unfamiliar but self-explanatory term.
Tony smiled before elaborating.

"Conflict-resolution is all the rage in American
schools right now, sir," he went on.

Now it was Hiawatha's turn to raise his eyebrows,
which he did upon hearing Tony address the policeman so formally and respectfully. Hiawatha had never
used the word "sir" in his entire life; his own father,
an avid authoritarian, had never pushed his son quite
so far, at least not linguistically. Tony continued.

"You see, the girls were always calling each
other names. I'm not sure which one started it all,

but Professor Musing and I both suspect it was Kimberly Ann. She was the more erratic of the two, and the more changeable. Ruthie, whatever else she was, was pretty consistent."

"Was there ever any violence?" asked Inspector Greene, as though pausing momentarily in the act of daintily sipping up these details through a drinking straw—an incongruous image, given the width of the detective's mouth and the fleshiness of his lips.

"No," said Tony, nodding for confirmation in the direction of Hiawatha, "at least not as far as we were aware. It was mainly name-calling and goading, as I've said. Until, that is, the night they died."

"Yes, yes, the dinner party. I've heard a little about it from some of the others. Quite a showdown, I take it."

Inspector Greene had in fact heard more than a little about the previous evening, with its lavish, bacchanalian banquet culminating in the wrestling match between Ruthie and Kimberly Ann. It was the one topic upon which, naturally enough, all the students had tended to focus in their brief statements. Interestingly, it had been played down by the foundress of the feast, Lady Elevenish. The policeman was curious to hear what the current discussants made of it all. For the latest detailed account, Tony now deferred to Hiawatha.

"Well," Hi began, taking a deep breath, and swallowing painfully. "Ruthie was a tiny bit late for dinner, and when she came into the dining room, Kimberly Ann sort of teased her, pretending to think that Ruthie wouldn't recognize what the plates were for . . ."

Hi gave a lengthy description of the meal, including precise information concerning the specific dishes served, for the notable ingredients of which the detective made frequent interruptions. After recounting the climactic, explosive collision between Ruthie and Kimberly Ann, in a rousing style worthy of Kipling (for, in spite of his resolve not to get carried away, Hiawatha found himself quite passionate in the retelling), the speaker actually seemed exhausted, his colleague impressed, the detective satisfied. But the interview was not yet over. Superintendent Greene interlaced his fingers over his fat middle and pondered quietly before proceeding.

"Well, there seems to be some suggestion of motive there," he said, in his most resonant and Churchillian tone. "Perhaps too much motive. But of course, they didn't kill each other. I suppose Miss Slatt could have killed Miss Crestview and then killed herself in shame or out of fear. Tell me, how did the rest of the students feel about this rivalry?"

"Well, sir, it's a funny thing," offered Tony. "I think most of them were amused by it all. Not that we approved of that. But to tell the truth, it was almost a galvanizing factor. Almost as though the mutual repulsion of the two girls brought the others closer together."

"None of the other students had problems with either Miss Slatt or Miss Crestview?"

Tony and Hi turned to one another, then both shook their heads.

"Well, there are still so many things that must be clarified. For instance, the other students all claim to have been in their beds by midnight, or shortly there-after. If the forensic physician is correct in his prelimi-nary investigations—and I've known Dr. Steers for a decade, and I can assure you that he is correct—Miss Crestview was killed no earlier than two o'clock in the morning. We know from numerous easily-identified— I suppose I must call them 'clues'—that there was some sort of a struggle, and that the body was moved from the window to the bed. How is it possible that nobody heard anything? And most puzzling of all, how could —" here he looked down at a little notepad he had silently withdrawn from his jacket "—how could Miss Simon not have heard anything in the next bed? If, as she says, she was in bed by one o'clock?"

Tony Trefthven-Woooser seemed to turn a shade paler at the mention of Paula Simon. Hiawatha, uncomfortable before this line of questioning even began, was becoming increasingly so.

"Well, I suppose it's possible that Paula made a mistake about the time. And as far as the noise, I didn't hear anything either." Tony seemed to be hesi-tating, and that was not at all like him.

"Yes, but in the same room with Miss Crest-view? Or immediately next door?" Here the inspector referred to his little black pad again. "Is it possible that neither . . . Michael Teller and Rupert Augustus nor . . . Miss Libby Moss, occupying the rooms adjacent to that shared by Miss Simon and Miss Crestview on either side, heard anything of the murderous commotion? Of course you, Mr. Trefthven-Woooser, were two rooms away, were you not?"

"Yes," said Tony, suddenly very pale indeed.

"In your own room? Isn't that correct?"

Tony exhaled loudly, before at last replying.

"Well, the fact is, I was two rooms away, as I've said. But I wasn't in my own room. I had moved, around midnight, to the room two doors down on the other side of Paula and Kimberly Ann. So you see, I was two rooms away, but on the other side."

Inspector Greene looked surprised, but at the same time it was clear that he intended his surprise to be recognized as false.

"Oh yes? And why did you change your room? Something naughty?"

Tony's complexion instantly ran the gamut from white to scarlet.

"Not at all, sir! I just found my bed a bit uncomfortable, and the reading lamp was inadequate. As I had some things to go through, I thought I would just hunt out a more convenient nest, so to speak. I had a feeling that Saul Raven's room would be empty, so I camped there."

"And what made you think that Mr. Raven's room would be empty?"

"Well, he tends to spend his time with one of the other students." Upon revealing this, Tony exchanged miserable, embarrassed looks with Hi, who was also becoming visibly agitated.

"Ah yes, now I remember," said the Detective Superintendent disingenuously, as again, it was obvious that whatever he claimed to have recalled, he had in fact never forgotten, "Mr. Raven said that he and Miss Moss always room together. Very refreshing, that straightforward American acknowledgment of cohabitation. Still, odd they didn't hear anything from Miss Moss's room. And you, Dr. Trefthven-Woooser, did anything unusual arise during your self-imposed nocturnal exile?"

"Nothing at all," said Tony with unveiled defensiveness.

"No visitors?"

Tony shook his head. Both he and Hiawatha were certain that the policeman had someone specific in mind when he asked this last question, but he offered them no clue as to what he meant. During the subsequent lull in the conversation, Hiawatha squirmed uncomfortably. Sensing that Inspector Greene was about to press him for details concerning his own whereabouts on the night of the murders, he became very anxious, almost delirious. It wasn't only himself he wanted to protect, he didn't want Lady Elevenish to look bad in the eyes of the police and, eventually no doubt, in the eyes of her husband. Hiawatha actually started to feel quite dizzy. He thought he would do anything to bring about an end to the conversation.

"Look here, Inspector," he said, adopting unconsciously some of his older interlocutor's parliamentarian mode of address, "I'm feeling rather sick. I wonder if we couldn't continue this later." Hiawatha considered that at the very least he must stall for time, until his sister Antigone arrived to advise him.

"Not feeling well?" said Superintendent Greene, as though this were somehow good news for him.

"As a matter of fact I'm feeling rather faint." And the truth was, Hiawatha was feeling exactly as he described.

"Well, I suppose, just as you Americans say, it's the squeaky wheel that gets the oil."

Hi was slightly taken aback by the policeman's skeptical, insinuating, and not altogether apt reply, so he tried to make light of the situation.

"As appealing as it is in theory, Superintendent, I am afraid that I must decline your offer to oil me."

It is impossible to say how this remark, intended in jest, was received by the heavy, sixty-year-old police chief; his face gave nothing away. But it did have the effect that Hiawatha and Tony both desired.

"Well, I can find you again after you've had a rest. At dinner, perhaps, to which Lady Elevenish has so kindly invited me. I do understand. It must all be quite a strain."

Superintendent Greene made this final admission warmly, but with his usual blank expression. Hiawatha straightened his legs in front of him prior to rising from his chair. Once he and Tony had both stood up to leave, the policeman added, in a different, much louder tone, and as though concluding a public address or official diplomatic statement,

"Nevertheless, we shall get to the bottom of it, make no mistake."

Hiawatha nodded farewell, and followed Tony to the door. They left the detective sitting on the sofa with his fingers at his lips, tugging on an imaginary cigar, defiantly flicking the ash in the general direction of Dresden.

VII

A WOMAN IN LOVE

(Notwithstanding the circumstances)

WHILE TONY AND HIAWATHA WERE UNDERGOING their second interrogation of the day, Lady Elevenish was walled up in her chamber like a queen after a scandalous affair involving herself and several members of the lesser nobility. On the advice of Superintendent Greene, Lucy had given the students freedom to explore the estate, with the stipulation that no one was to leave the grounds without the detective's express consent. Now, glancing occasionally out the largest of six great windows in her private sitting room, she saw the young people wandering singly or in small groups among the garden ornaments and greenhouses, their heads invariably lowered, their stride, without exception, slow and melancholy, like the figures in an evening landscape by Watteau.

"Poor things," said Lady Elevenish to her friends, Millie and Coral, who had walled themselves up with her like proper loyal handmaids.

"Yes, the poor dears," agreed Coral Marsden, taking her cue from her hostess in this as in most things. She was even dressed like Lady Elevenish today, in a long, cylindrical gown of deeply-hued velvet, meticulously pleated in the mode of Fortuny.

"Who are you talking about?" said Millie Dumont, without real interest. She was lounging on one of two *chaises longues* that flanked the tea table in Lady Elevenish's sanctuary. In neither her speech nor her costume was there any suggestion that she wished to emulate the mistress of Lostlindens; her accent was pure upper-East Side Manhattan, her outfit a custard-colored slack suit by Ralph Lauren. "Do you mean the police?" she continued, resuming her perusal of the real estate pages in the latest issue of *Country Life*.

Honestly, thought Lady Elevenish sourly, confronted by her friend's exasperating obtuseness. It was hardly surprising that Millie's mother had been a collector of paperweights, because her daughter had a mind like a lump of glass. For export only.

"No dear. Not the police. The students," she said, in her best imitation of Margaret Thatcher telling a lie about the ultimate beneficiaries of her proposed taxation policies. Then she added, rather emotionally, "And of coase the two teachers. I feel dreadfully sorry for them."

This was sincere, especially with regard to one of the two men. Like a college sophomore, Lady Elevenish was frankly dying to talk about the new and sudden love she felt for her young professorial houseguest, Hiawatha Musing, a love for which, she considered almost hopefully, her husband would undoubtedly kill her, kill them both perhaps. Not that Manfred himself had not indulged in similar dalliances with more than one pretty undergraduate who had sycophantically flattered him by expressing an interest in Richard Crashaw. And then there had been Lucy's one true rival, an odious Canadian scholar named Candace Hobnog who taught at The University of Ottawa and who had accumulated her own world-class collection of Crashaviana, to which she seemed sometimes inclined to add Sir Manfred. Lady Elevenish now entertained the provoking possibility, which had already occurred to her more than once, that the mannish, crane-necked Ms. Hobnog was also examining the New Zealand archives at that very moment. But then the exhilaration of her emotional reawakening burbled back over Lucy like the waters of baptism, and she felt drained of jealousy, felt in fact that she could not contain her joy.

"Well, let's not forget the dead girls in our pity," said Millie with a hint of sarcasm, while Lady Eleve- nish leaned pensively against the window sill, remind- ing herself, if no one else, of Wallis Simpson posing on the balcony at the Chateau de Candé. Perhaps Lucy, too, would be forced to suffer through a painful divorce. But she would never give up the house. She tried again to turn the conversation in the happier direction of Hiawatha.

"Tell me, what do you really think of these two professors? I'm curious to know your impressions."

Coral was first to speak.

"Well Mr. Trefthven-Woooser seemed very oblig- ing at dinner. Of coase, he was awfully fond of himself and his pedigree."

Lady Elevenish smiled approvingly at her friend's use of the very English phrase, "awfully fond of him- self." Coral was coming along nicely. But she her- self didn't want to waste time talking about Tony Trefthven-Woooser.

"And how about the other one? The American?" said Lucy, with studied nonchalance. "Don't you think he's rathah sweet?"

"I always thought 'Hiawatha' was a girl's name," laughed Millie coarsely, and Lucy could have struck her. She was about to point out the small spot of—cooking grease, was it?—on the knee of Mrs. Dumont's lovely slacks, when the opportunity for revenge was snatched from her by a knock on the sitting room door. Lady Elevenish opened it to find her butler, his old, laconic self again after the discombobulations of the morning.

"Well M'm," said Feathers, with a flinty eye.

Lucy stared back blankly. Feathers ventured a tiny bit further.

"The Police Superintendent . . ." Here he stopped, as if he clearly thought these spare words were more than enough to discharge his duty.

Like a contestant on a television game show, Lucy made an excited guess at his meaning.

"Oh, you mean the Inspector wants to see me?" She was thrilled when Feathers nodded gravely, because she wanted to get away from her unsympathetic friends, upon whom her innuendoes of romantic rebirth fell as on mute stones.

Bidding a perfunctory farewell to these as-yet unenlightened confidantes, Lucy Elevenish sped off toward the morning room. She was hoping to arrive before Hiawatha, about whose interview with Inspector Greene she had been informed in advance, had left. In this she was disappointed. When she came upon the gelatinous policeman, he was alone, in the same place Tony and Hi had left him, staring thoughtfully at the picture of Lady Georgiana doing her dance with the harebells and ferns.

"Remarkable likeness, Lady Lucy," said Superintendent Greene, when she had seated herself opposite him.

"Yes," she murmured in reply, graciously acknowledging what she supposed was the standard compliment.

"But badly cleaned, I think," continued the policeman.

This rejoinder confused Lady Elevenish slightly, and put her off.

"You wished to have a word with me, Mr. Greene?" said Lucy, with just a touch of *hauteur*, to bring the detective back to the purpose of the present meeting.

Superintendent Greene dropped his eyes to the level of the speaker. When he addressed her, it was with much the same pompous manner he had adopted earlier for the interrogation of Hiawatha and Tony, the only alteration being the addition of a slight chivalrous deference which invariably informed his treatment of the fairer sex.

"Lady Elevenish, I hope you won't mind my asking you a few questions. Of course I hate to distract you from the burdensome duties of hostess, which you must feel now more than ever, under these trying circumstances."

Lucy wished the detective would come to the point. Still, she allowed him to impose his own conversational rhythm, while she maintained her characteristic formal aloofness, with the addition of a slight, almost tangible vulnerability which invariably informed her behavior toward the rougher sex.

"Lady Elevenish," continued Detective Greene, picking a speck of lint from his lapel. "I hope you will excuse my frankness when I ask you, what on earth are all of these people doing in your house?"

Lady Elevenish actually approved his frankness.

"Oh, you want to know why I'm hosting a houseful of American students? That's simple enough. My husband, Sir Manfred" (after only two years of referring to her spouse by his title, and in spite of the many ways in which her marriage clearly fell short of her ideals, Lady Elevenish always glowed with satisfaction when she spoke these words), "Sir Manfred was visiting a college in the United States not long ago, in Illinois, to be precise. He was receiving an honorary degree. And during the ceremony, he was seated on the dais next to the president of the college, and they got to talking and, well, next thing you know, he's invited the president to send some of their pupils to us. I'm afraid—I mean, I'm proud—to say it was my idea that they spend a weekend. So much nicer for them than flying through like tourists."

"That's very generous of you, Your Ladyship. Very ambassadorial, to be sure. But tell me, don't they pay anything for their visit?"

Lucy winced, as though a sensitive tooth had been discovered by a dentist's tool. The Lorimer money that was paying for the restoration of Lostlindens had not been made by giving things away.

"Well, yes, as a matter of fact, they pay a small sum, to cover a few of the expenses, which are considerable, as you will easily imagine."

Detective Greene relinquished this line of questioning. The financial arrangement between the American program and the Elevenishes played no actual part in his investigation, but was a subject of his own personal curiosity. Now that that curiosity was satisfied, he moved on to more pertinent topics.

"Other than your friends, Coral Marsden and Millie Dumont," he said, referring to his small notebook as before, "you had never encountered any of your guests prior to this visit? Is that correct?"

"Well, in fact, coincidentally, I have met one of them before. Professor Musing. We were at a party together, when I visited the States a couple of years ago." She was tempted to add, 'Don't you think he's dreamy?' The idea made even her smile. She had to tell someone, though perhaps not Detective Greene. "Why do you ask?" she went on more seriously, after a thoughtful pause.

Detective Greene seemed not to have heard her question.

"What time did you go to your bed last night?"

Lady Elevenish blushed ever so briefly.

"Oh, I would say around midnight, perhaps a little after."

"Did you remain in your own rooms till this morning?"

"Yes, Inspector, I did," declared Lucy, with some vehemence. And it was the truth.

"I hope you'll forgive me, Lady Elevenish," continued the circumspect Mr. Greene. "I have reason to believe that there was a great deal of movement in this house long after midnight last night, and it is perfectly logical to conclude that some of that movement 'took in' or, in other words, encompassed—if you see my point—the violent acts which we are left to decipher today."

"Well," said Lady Elevenish, the Texan rising within her like mercury in a barometer, "as you know, my own rooms are in the opposite wing of the house from the guest wing. I could hardly have heard anything from where I was." She was suddenly suspicious of the reasons for the police chief's questions.

"Yes, yes, I trust you implicitly," he assured her, which naturally made Lady Elevenish wonder why, if it was implicit, he had bothered to make the point aloud. He went on, rather confidentially.

"Lady Elevenish, I have reason to think that even the two instructors did some—what shall we call it?—bed-hopping last night. Mr. Trefthven-Woooser has just admitted as much. And I believe Professor Musing was about to make a similar confession when he was taken ill." He waited to see Lucy's reaction to this news.

Lady Elevenish, for her part, tried to twist her face ever so slightly in order to express surprise, but only the mildest variety. More disturbing than the detective's revelation concerning Hiawatha's displacement during the night, which was of course no revelation to her, was his use of the term "confession." What on earth was this great grey pudding of a policeman trying to suggest? She decided to allow him to continue speaking, restricting her reaction to a weak smile.

"Your Ladyship," continued Mr. Greene, "one of the students has generously told us about the incident which occurred upon the group's arrival at your stately home."

"Incident?" she mimicked, like a dowager on the stage.

"Yes, having to do with the famous Shakespeare boot. A relic cherished not only by you and your husband and his ancestors, but by all the people living in the environs of Camford, including, I may add, your humble servant, which is to say, myself."

"Yes, but I don't see what this incident —" Lady Elevenish interjected, with genuine curiosity.

"This forthcoming student stated that Miss Ruthie Slatt had been reprimanded by Professor Musing for having tried on the boot. That the reprimand seemed to have embarrassed her."

"Yes, well I doubt the young woman was capable of embarrassment, but I must say that Professor Musing handled her very gently. And he saved me having to make a long lecture."

Inspector Greene considered Lady Elevenish's assessment of the situation.

"Would you say, granting your limited familiarity with his character, that Professor Musing was under a visible strain in supervising these two very unruly students, Ruthie Slatt and Kimberly Ann Crestview? Perhaps even that he resented this duty, and the deceased girls themselves?"

Lady Elevenish found herself, all at once, extremely angry. Here she was in love for the first time in thirty years—perhaps for ever, for all she could remember of being young—and this fat English bloodhound was going to tell her that it was a no-go, that her tiny windfall of hope and happiness was canceled, that the object of her momentous affection was soon to be carted off to jail. It was monstrous. It was laughable, of course, but also unfair, above all to her.

"I think, Inspector, you must be out of your mind, if you are saying what I think you're saying," she said at last, with great dignity and restraint.

Inspector Greene smiled as though he had played his hand perfectly.

"Well, I suppose we can discuss these things again, at dinner. As a matter of fact, Lady Lucy, I was hoping you might help me to organize a more general meeting this evening, after we've eaten of course. Everybody—students, teachers, household staff—all together. Then I could explain a few of our procedures, and tell you what we know, and what more we need to know. It would be so helpful. And in this way, there would be no troublesome spread of rumors of the sort that cause unnecessary anxiety and even suffering."

Lucy realized that she was herself suffering at this moment, and everything in her character rebelled at the notion that it was necessary. She wanted to rush out of the room to look for Hiawatha, to warn him of the detective's suspicions—however far-fetched—and to calm what she knew would be his terrified reaction. But there was still a practical issue to resolve with the police chief.

"Detective Greene," she spoke after he had finished outlining his plans for the evening. "I wonder if you realize that the group is scheduled to leave

Lostlindens tomorrow morning, to begin their two-week stay at Woodbridge College?"

"Impossible," came the ponderous reply. "No one is to leave the house and grounds until we know better where we stand. I am fully aware that this will put you out somewhat, Your Ladyship, but I'm sure you will agree that, temporarily at least, it is what must be."

Lucy was visibly disturbed by this announcement. She had not planned to have fifteen guests beyond the weekend. Of course, it would allow her additional time with Hiawatha, but she had already arranged in her mind that, after the group had departed, Hiawatha could be ferried back and forth from Woodbridge College by her chauffeur, Dustin, a raffish, snickering widower for whom an excuse to park his vehicle near the undergraduate residence halls would be as good as a paid holiday. Still, she didn't like the idea of being forced to put up the younger crowd indefinitely, though Superintendent Greene was clearly capable of enforcing his will. She decided, in the end, and in her eagerness to get away and find Hi, that she would accept this decision for now, saying only that she hoped it wouldn't be for too long. As this seemed to have brought their conversation to a conclusion, Lucy stood up to leave, when Detective Greene abruptly raised a heavy hand.

"Oh there is one more thing," he said. "The coach driver, Mr. MacMenzies? When was the last time you saw him?"

"I don't think I've ever actually seen him, since the group arrived. Mrs. Shant—she's my cook—looked after him. Why?"

"No urgency," replied Mr. Greene, quite mystifyingly. And then Lucy made her hasty exit from her own favorite room in the house, without so much as a parting glance at her favorite picture.

Making her way to the guest wing, Lucy found herself outside of Hiawatha's door. She felt she must speak with him, to warn him about the insinuating questions posed by the police chief, and to kiss him just once, for hours had passed since their last embrace. She knocked softly on the door, and a weak, hoarse voice responded from within.

"Who is it?"

"It's me," whispered Lady Lucy, tremblingly turning the knob.

She came upon Hiawatha lying in bed, in the dark, his pale face hovering above the counterpane like a worried moon struggling out of the sea. In a flash, Lady Elevenish was sitting next to him on the bed.

"How are you feeling, my dear?" she whispered again, giddy with the sensation that when they were together, she was not herself, the sham-English aristocrat, nor even her old, half-forgotten self, the girlish and ambitious Lucille Lorimer, but someone altogether new.

"I'm a little better, I think. Mrs. Shant brought me something to drink."

Lucy could well imagine what Mrs. Shant had provided, and it would certainly help to numb his discomfort. Her own contribution to this cause was to lie down next to him, on top of the bedclothes, and speak softly in his ear.

"I've missed you all day," she said. "And I'm worried about you."

Hiawatha withstood these ministrations, neither encouraging nor rejecting her.

"Oh, I'll be all right," he sighed, swallowing hard. "It's only a cold, after all. Though I suppose it could be pneumonia." Then he added gently, "You know, it's very kind of you to think about me."

This broke Lucy's heart, but she had more to say.

"My dear, of course I will always think about you. But I must warn you, too. Superintendent Greene seems to think you've been up to something. Naturally I didn't say you were with me last night. But he seemed to be suspicious of you. I had to come and tell you to be careful with him."

Through the haze provided by Mrs. Shant, Hiawatha found it hard to muster the nervousness that such news would normally have instilled in him. He was in any case not unprepared to hear that the detective was speculating as to his whereabouts on the previous night.

"Yes, I felt the same thing, when Tony and I talked to him. And then, after we'd gone, Tony confessed to me that, earlier today, he had mentioned to one of the policemen that he had tried to find me around one last night, but that I wasn't in my room. He felt pretty badly about it at the time, but now he feels terrible, as though he'd done me a great deal of harm. Ironic, too, since he subsequently admitted to Greene that he wasn't in his own room, either."

Lady Elevenish was very angry at Trefthven-Woooser, and less inclined to believe in his contrition, but she didn't want to upset Hi. So instead of prolonging the unpleasantness of the past several hours, she decided to try and console her friend. She was in the middle of removing her rings to the bedside table, with the intention of getting into the bed with Hi, when there was a knock on the door, and she sat bolt upright.

"Who is it?" said Hiawatha, his voice suggesting the extremity to which fatigue had brought him.

The door opened. It was Feathers, the soundless and all-seeing.

"A Mrs. Antigone Musing Vanderlyn, M'Lady."

"Tig!" cried Hiawatha, springing from his bed, fully clothed. And, with Lady Elevenish running after him, he hastened down the great staircase toward the hall, to welcome his sister.

VIII

ANTIGONE EX MACHINA

*(Including information coincidentally
and sympathetically obtained)*

WELL, YOU'VE REALLY STEPPED INTO IT THIS TIME," said the young woman, smiling to show that her summons at such short notice and in such peculiar circumstances presented no particular difficulties for her.

Antigone Vanderlyn, née Musing, opened the suitcase she had hastily filled only ten hours earlier, curious to see what she had packed. Her brother Hiawatha, still in his stocking feet, stood watching her, dazzled at just how radiantly she proved the old adage about pregnancy making women more beautiful. Always considered good-looking, Tig now appeared to have attained to a pinnacle of personal attractiveness, as though she had entered a phase for which she was, physically speaking at least, intended by nature. She had always been, for her brother, a living symbol—in fact *the* symbol—of intelligence and reliability, a combination even rarer than might be supposed, and now those qualities and others seemed perfectly aligned with or reflected by her external features: the lovely face, formerly tending to paleness, now pink and glowing, the dark eyes, often tired from research and grading, now refreshed and eager, the whole image brought once and for all into vivid focus which the slightest alteration would presumably blur.

Brother and sister were standing in the bedroom to which Lady Elevenish had personally conducted them upon Antigone's arrival. Anxious to guarantee Hiawatha's happiness, and by extension her own, Lady Elevenish had of course insisted that Antigone take up residence at the house with her pneumonic sibling. In fact, the mistress of Lostlindens had greeted her newest guest as though they were already sisters-in-law, an attitude which Hiawatha noted and which made him more than a little uneasy.

"Oh but you must stay here with us," Lady Elevenish had rung out in the ancient hall, wrapping her arms around Tig's very slightly distended waist, in a most sisterly-in-law fashion.

"But will that be all right? I mean, will the police allow it?" inquired Tig, as they made their way toward the stairs.

"Of course, the police will do eggsoooahctly what they're told," said Lady Elevenish with conviction, opting rather arbitrarily and as at short notice for her most British manner. "Now I myself will show you to your room, and on the way you must tell me about that husband of yours. How well I remember seeing you together when we met in Massachusetts. Anyone could tell you were the apple of his eye."

And what am I? A juice-orange? thought Hiawatha, following the two women up the great stairs. Hiawatha was in fact fond enough of his brother-in-law, the famous archeologist, Cornelius Vanderlyn, but that fondness had been achieved only after a struggle, since Hi was one of those brothers who instinctively resent any males who marry into the family.

Having shown her automatic, almost proprietary, interest in anything and anyone connected to Hiawatha, Lady Elevenish confirmed her intentions to keep her lover's sister in the house with a loud and impressive display of aristocratic pique, making short work of the police sergeant who questioned her authority to admit new guests to the crime scene. After taking her bows for this performance, and establishing a chummy if not positively familial atmosphere among the three of them, Lucy rather begrudgingly left Hiawatha and Antigone alone in the latter's commodious bedroom, and went off to make the last-minute dinner arrangements with her cook.

"Hold on a moment!" exclaimed Tig suddenly, when she and Hi were alone. "This isn't one of the dead girls' rooms, is it?"

Hi groaned at the thought that his sister needed to use the plural possessive. Then he reassured her.

"Good God no!"

Hiawatha sank into a chintz-covered chair before the window. Antigone, withdrawing articles of her clothing from the suitcase, studied him discreetly. He certainly didn't look well, which was understandable in the circumstances. But Tig knew that she must try to keep him from brooding, at least until she could get him away from Lostlindens, the scene of the bizarre tragedy, though, as she gathered from Lucy Elevenish, such an escape would not be possible in the immediate future.

"Well, I guess that's the end of *English Life in Literature*," she said after a long pause, without the least hint of mockery, but as a prelude to what might otherwise seem a too clinical inquiry into the details of the crimes. Antigone was a scientist, and as such keenly interested in all the facts surrounding the strange double death. Moreover, like her brother, she possessed the heightened curiosity of the born sleuth, both having discovered this shared inclination when they were involved in solving the murder of Cornelius Vanderlyn's first wife.

"Oh Tig, you can't imagine what it's been like these past twenty-four hours," said Hiawatha, launching into a lengthy and surprisingly coherent account of the revelations of the morning, and then tracing them back to the events of the previous night, and of the restless days and nights that went before. He seemed, in his impassioned descriptions of various incidents, and of his own despairing reactions to them, to have forgotten about his cold; in any case, the breathless flow of his story was uninterrupted by sneeze or cough. By the time he finally paused—as it seemed, for air—Tig had seated herself in a chair opposite her brother, duly horrified by his predicament but intrigued by the puzzle as well. When Hi had covered every conceivable aspect of the situation, providing exhaustively-detailed portraits of all the students on the course, recreating at great length the more noteworthy interactions between them, and lastly drawing up a verbal plan of the guest wing of Lostlindens and the division of the rooms among the lodgers, another long silence ensued. Tig was deciding how to express her commiseration in such a way as to convince Hiawatha that they must now be constructive, specifically by beginning their own investigation of the mysterious deaths, when Hi spoke up again.

"And that's not all, Tig."

"Oh," she responded, with a worried look to match his own.

"No. I mean, yes. The fact is, I think I'm having an affair with Lucy Elevenish."

Tig's jaw dropped.

"What do you mean you think you're having an affair?" The news had certainly taken her by surprise.

"That is to say, we've done things, but I can't remember exactly what," replied Hi, apparently more confused than embarrassed by his relationship with the lady of the house.

"Hiawatha!" said Antigone, in a perfect imitation of their mother at her most exasperated. She was not angry that Hi might be having an affair with a married woman, so much as that he wasn't certain whether he was or not.

"Well whatever it was, it was an accident. She kept plying me with wine."

Tig raised her eyebrows and Hiawatha raced on.

"The truth is, Tig, I've been so tense about this course, this bloody course."

"Well, Hi, if you're using words like 'bloody' then clearly you are having an affair with her, because that's pure Lucy Elevenish if I remember her rightly."

Despite his sister's reliable deduction, it still remained a blur to Hiawatha, exactly what had happened last night. He had certainly been a bit drunk, and now, all he was capable of conjuring up by way of recollection was an image of his old cat rolling in the wild mint leaves back in his parents' garden in Boston.

"And so, you see, it complicates matters, because, though I haven't yet had an opportunity to explain it all to Superintendent Greene—you'll love him, by the way; he's like the secret offspring of Winston Churchill and Dame Edna, very pompous and very probing, and he looks a bit like both of them—the fact that I wasn't in my own room when the murder or murders—they're still not sure how Ruthie died—took place. And Lucy, I mean of course Lady Elevenish, tells me that Greene thinks I resented both students, and was under some sort of strain when everything happened as it did. You'll have to explain to him, Tig, that I've been under a strain since I was two. This would be the first time it's driven me to murder. As far as we know."

Antigone smiled and relaxed further into her chair. Hiawatha, too, whatever he might have said to the contrary, felt suddenly calm. He had upturned his pitcher of troubles into his sister's capacious glass, without holding back so much as a single drop of anxiety. Since childhood, the sharing of responsibility and strength in adversity had been the basis of their sibling relationship. The sympathy that joined them was deep and impenetrable and beyond the fraying grasp of worldly calamity. This needed no proof when they were together; it had often been proved when they were apart. After all, Tig happily reminded herself now, had not her brother suffered from nausea, and known that she was pregnant, several weeks before she found out herself? Antigone's love for her husband, Cornelius, was a source of unending wonder to her, a thrilling place where desire and a host of less easily named emotions vivified her body as they revealed to her her mind. But her love for Hiawatha was an older love and, for all of his often worrisome sadness, a fount of quiet and familiar peace.

"Dear Hi," she said at last, as an alternative to becoming too sentimental, which Musings had a horror of being, "don't think for a moment that you're the only one who's got interesting news."

Hiawatha was instantly ashamed.

"Oh no! I haven't asked you at all about the baby, and Cornelius of course, and how you're doing."

"The baby and I and Cornelius are all doing very well, thank you. But that's not what I'm talking about. You'll never guess who was on the plane with me."

Hiawatha loved to guess.

"Mick Jagger? Claus von Bulow? Bidu Sayao?"

"Yes, but aside from them," she said, taunting him as she always did.

"I'm altogether stumped," said her brother.

"Does the name 'Miranda Wilpool Crestview Frink' mean anything to you?" She knew very well that it would.

"Are you serious? You were on the same plane with Kimberly Ann's mother?"

"Yes," said Tig, rather proud of her luck, but especially of the opportunity it had provided her for interrogation. "The poor woman lives with her second—or is it her third?—husband in Boston. Naturally she was quite upset."

"At me, I suppose," said Hi morosely, "for killing her daughter."

Tig frowned, a traditional first step toward bucking her brother up.

"Not at all. You see, we were sitting quite close to one another in the waiting area before boarding the plane, and I noticed this rather heavyset, expensively-dressed woman dabbing at her eyes and looking very distraught, and so I turned to her and asked her if I could be of some help. We got to talking, and when she explained the sad reason for her journey, well, naturally I told her who I was. She seemed glad to have someone to talk to, started telling me all about her little Kimmy Ann, and how she was always afraid something like this would happen to her. What do you think of that?"

Hiawatha could not help being intrigued by the idea that Kimberly Ann's own mother had her pegged for a murder victim. Or was that just the normal maternal concern for the safety of the fledglings?

"Go on, what else did she say?"

"Well," Tig took a deep breath, which heightened the rosy color in her cheeks. "She said that nobody had ever really understood her little girl. Now, as teachers, we both know that when a parent claims his or her child is misunderstood, it always means there's been trouble. But of course I couldn't come right out and ask her what kind of trouble Kimberly Ann had been in. Fortunately, she took my silence at that point as a gentle indication that I at least would try to understand her daughter, even if it was too late to help her. It was truly heartbreaking to hear Mrs. Frink talk, and I felt guiltily conscious of noting everything she said, for future reference."

"But what did she tell you?" Hi hastened his sister on.

"The poor woman claimed in no uncertain terms that her ex-husband, Kimberly Ann's father, had always heartlessly blamed his own little girl for her parents' divorce. Nevertheless, after the divorce, twelve-year-old Kimberly Ann had opted to stay in Baltimore with Mr. Crestview, rather than go to Boston with her mother and her younger sister—when she mentioned this, the woman seemed a bit tense, though she had stopped crying—and there had been some trouble with one of her father's lady friends. I couldn't make out all the details, but at some point a pair of scissors entered the story—and the upper thigh of the lady friend."

Antigone took a moment to let her brother appreciate what she felt was this happy turn of phrase. Hi made a blank face, as though he didn't quite understand. Tig explained.

"That is, the friend of Kimberly Ann's father wound up in the hospital after having a fight with daddy's little girl."

"What else?" inquired Hi, greedy for more information.

"That was all we had time for. We were separated when we boarded the plane; she was in first class and I was in coach. I fell asleep before we took off, and didn't wake up till after we'd landed. Very refreshing."

"And Mrs. Frink?" asked Hi avidly.

"When we were going through customs in London, I deliberately caught up with her again. By then she seemed to have collected herself somewhat, and she treated me a little more coolly than before. But she did say that the police were coming to meet her, to take her to the Bothwick Arms, the local inn, where I would have stayed if your new reason for living, Lady Elevenish, had not insisted upon putting me up here with you. And a good thing, too."

Hi blushed again and then threw himself into a violent fit of coughing. When he was done, Antigone leaned nearer to him and asked in a very serious, searching tone, "Do you think you might love this woman?"

Hiawatha was tempted to laugh, which would have been callous, perhaps, but he also realized that he would, after all, be laughing at himself. He looked miserable and said nothing.

"I do wish we could begin to figure out what might make you happy," said Tig, and she instantly realized that her hormones were playing tiddly-winks with her emotions. So she drew herself up, adopting the cordial but never desperate manner of a bank teller or telephone operator inquiring after necessary information.

"Are you ever happy, Hi? I know it isn't easy right now, but sometimes?"

"Well it's funny you should ask," said Hiawatha, "but every once in a while when I'm lying in my bed I feel this strange warmth, as though there were a little flame inside me, kind of like a pilot light, just below my heart but not as low as my stomach, flickering, just to remind me it's there. I think that might be my happiness, the little hope that happiness exists." Then, sensing he was losing his sister, or worse, perhaps depressing her, he answered less obscurely,

"And of course I'm happy that you're here."

The moment was snatched from them by the distant sound of the dinner gong.

IX

BLINDMAN'S BUFF

*(In which a greater number of mysteries are
made known than in any chapter heretofore)*

DINNER THAT SECOND EVENING AT LOSTLINDENS
was a comparatively tight-lipped, even dour,
affair. No doubt this was at least partly due to the fact
that the two loosest-lipped, most raucous participants
in the previous evening's meal were no longer available for dining, much less providing entertainment by
their outrageous, impromptu antics. However complex and various the emotions they may have aroused
in their classmates when they were alive, Kimberly
Ann and Ruthie clearly left a gap when they departed,
and the quiet resulting from their absence rather poi-
gnantly resembled, if it was not in actual fact on the
sincerest level, mourning among the survivors. In

any case, a distinctly funereal—not to say somewhat spooky—air pervaded the banqueting saloon, such that to an outsider the gathering must have appeared more a séance than a group repast, presided over by an unlikely medium in the corpulent, ponderously gregarious person of Police Chief Clive Cornwallis Greene.

Throughout the meal, despite attempts on the part of the Superintendent to draw them out with his own lighthearted reflections on what he knew of American customs, the students remained sullen and unresponsive. Blighted, they seemed, like a bed of brightly-colored flowers caught off guard by an untimely frost. And of course they could not help thinking of themselves now as prisoners; perhaps they were even in danger. Antigone, seated directly next to the police chief, felt that the students, to each of whom Hiawatha had introduced her at the outset of the meal, were smart to say as little as possible to the wily inspector, at least until he had explained how he was going to proceed. Opposite his sister, Hiawatha, his cold now full-blown, kept up as best he could a conversation with Lady Elevenish, whose number one priority he continued to be. Next to him, Tony Trefthven-Woooser made numerous attempts to capture Lady Elevenish's attention; he hardly succeeded in catching her eye. Lucy's friends, Millie Dumont and

Coral Marsden, carried on their own private conversation at the other end of the table, as if this were one of those restaurants where, according to a tradition of space-saving or democratic seating ideas, complete strangers find themselves sharing a single board.

As for the younger guests, they indulged in only the most perfunctory and guarded discourse, each wondering when they would be allowed to escape to their own rooms again. Rupert Augustus glared suspiciously at Paula Simon, whose tired, harried expression made it clear that she felt most vulnerable to suspicion, which indeed she was, at least from the detective's point of view, having yet to explain where she had spent the previous night. Sarah and Mame were remarkably quiet, exchanging few comments even between themselves, and Libby and Saul, too, though they never lost physical contact with one another, were only very seldom connected by speech. Molly, seated as usual between Herman and Paul, tried more than once to lure them into conversation, but gave up after she realized, with a little perturbed blush, that neither one seemed the least bit interested in what she had to say. As though to fill the vacuum created by all this reticence, Michael Teller was in fact the only person in the room who talked in a normal tone of voice, making a number of speculative remarks in between forkfuls of free-range veal.

"Well when I spoke to my parents today," he said at one point, "they told me that the story had already made the newspapers in Chicago, and they seemed rather proud that I was involved. Of course, they were also a bit worried. I assume, Superintendent Greene, that we will be allowed to leave here before long?"

"Oh yes, I imagine you will all be on your way soon," replied the detective, in a sing-song voice made even more mellow by the burgundy to which he had frequent recourse. And then he smiled almost flirtatiously at Antigone on his left; she, having consumed no alcohol, was unequipped to requite his inviting look.

"Not that I want to go back home right away," continued Michael. "I mean, we are going to continue the course, are we not? I for one am certainly looking forward to staying in Camford, '. . . gold-spired city of schoolboy reveries/ and refuge of the old man's remembering heart,' to quote Gray. Say, by the way, can you imagine what Ruthie would have said about us eating veal?"

No one rose to the challenge of this question. In fact, the mention of Ruthie rendered the others even quieter than before, so that Michael himself eventually conceded to the larger community's selection of silence as the appropriate atmosphere for the meal. It is to be noted, however, that while this grim state of affairs persisted, everyone nevertheless displayed

a healthy appetite, and most of the students had seconds of the Black Forest gâteau for dessert.

When they had finished eating, Detective Greene
rose up slowly like a hot-air balloon and announced
that everyone present was cordially required to attend
a special meeting to be held shortly in the so-called Chinese sitting room. At this news, several of the students
looked aghast, the rest of them, either uncertain or
utterly vacant. Still, they all turned up in the appointed
place at the appointed time. If at dinner they had
drooped, now, standing about the sizable parlor, they
seemed like a showroom of mechanical figures, from
each of which the energy source had been removed.
English Life in Literature was no longer a lively group
of enthusiastic young scholars, but a tableau of that
group, from which the souls of the individuals had
apparently run away to hide. Hiawatha well understood how they felt. He felt exactly the same: empty,
and yet, somehow, still afraid. While Lady Elevenish
anxiously stayed close to him, he stayed close to Antigone, who had remained silent throughout the meal,
exchanging only the most superficial politenesses with
Detective Greene. The latter, now perched unpreten-
tiously if somewhat precariously on a red leather
ottoman at one end of the room, surrounded by wall
murals intended to imitate the lacquer decorations
on chinoiserie furniture—fantasy landscapes in gold

against a black background—looked like a bulging porcelain Buddha produced for the Western market.

"Ladies and gentlemen, I've called you together in order to explain what we know about the terrible events of last night. You above all have every right and reason to be informed. After I have elucidated matters as they stand, I shall be asking you, in the presence of your supervisors and peers, a few things which will, I hope, help to expedite the resolution of this situation and your own departure for new and no doubt happier destinations."

Lucy Elevenish, who felt strongly that the deaths of two young people, however irregular and disturbing, in no way diminished the claim of Lostlindens to be the happiest conceivable destination, showed her disdain for the pompous detective in a wide, rather lurid smile. Motioning to Feathers, who was at the back of the room, she interrupted the police chief in an icy tone.

"Mr. Greene, I think we had awl better sit down, if you dewn't mind. Feathers will produce a few more chairs, if the students could be troubled to help bring them in. We cahn't begin yet anyway, because Mrs. Shant and the bus driver have not yet arrived."

Like the Witch of Endor called up from the depths by Saul, Mrs. Shant appeared in the doorway, still wearing her rubber gloves, her large nose a rubicund glow.

"Well, Your Ladyship," replied Greene, with an exaggerated show of satisfaction, "I'm very happy that you mention Mr. MacMenzies, because he has in fact been missing since some time last night. Has anyone here seen him?"

The detective scanned the room, a sea of shaking heads.

"Well, then, let us put aside for the time being the case of the disappearing coach driver, and concentrate our mental energies on the tragic deaths of Ruthie Slatt and Kimberly Ann Crestview." Here, rolling his eyes upward like a martyr invoking divine aid, the detective withdrew his standard attribute, the small black notebook, from his jacket pocket. "We now know that Ruthie Slatt died at approximately two o'clock this morning, after the fatal ingestion of one or more chemical substances, the precise identification of which is currently under way. So far, we can say that the contents of her stomach confirm she ate the same foods that we know to have been served at dinner, beginning with the melon soup and ending with a variety of sweets. Yes, that's right, we can even tell the order in which the foods were consumed."

Here the policeman paused, allowing his listeners time to appreciate the cunning and thoroughness of the forensic scientists on his team. Not one of the students, however, was eager to consider the contents of Ruthie Slatt's stomach, and several of them felt increasingly queasy as the detective went on.

"We may of course find out that drugs were involved."

A wave of uneasiness passed over the crowded room, which seemed momentarily like a stockholders meeting at which the director of the board, Mr. Greene, had announced a distasteful likelihood that dividends were no longer to be paid. But the detective did not, at this point, dwell on any single possible aspect of the crimes.

"Perhaps the most surprising detail of Ruthie's death was not what we found in her stomach, but what was found in her rucksack. When she died, Miss Slatt was in possession of thirty-eight thousand pounds sterling, in fifty-pound notes. Now I know all Americans are rich, but do you always carry such sums in cash? More importantly, did any of you know that Ruthie carried that kind of money around?"

"If I had known, I would have been nicer to her," said Herman Wadkin without thinking, but not actually in jest. The students, who were surprised and impressed by Ruthie's personal worth at the time of her death, were also embarrassed by Herman's candor, though Molly nearly giggled aloud.

"No one knew anything about that? No? All right, let's turn now to Miss Crestview. Kimberly

Ann Crestview seems to have died at very nearly the same time as Ruthie Slatt. Kimberly Ann's death, however, was the result of a more violent physical act. To be precise, she was strangled, most likely with a thin wire, though the actual weapon has not yet been found. What was found, however, was quite telling, namely, a rock that seems to have been thrown through one of the small panes of glass in her room." Here the detective produced, in a small plastic bag also removed from his pocket, a stone, roughly four inches in diameter, altogether lacking in geologic interest, and yet instantly the focal point of all eyes present. "A room, I should say, shared by Miss Crestview and you, Miss Simon," With this he shifted his head in order to scrutinize Paula, who turned abruptly away. "Though the room was, I understand, originally assigned to Miss Simon and Miss Slatt. What a bunch of jumping beans you students are!"

Whether this remark, spoken with a smile, was meant solely as a pleasantry or something more probing is unknown. At any rate, no one in the room resembled a jumping bean at that moment, transfixed as everybody was by the police chief's narration.

"During a painstaking search of the house, conducted by myself and eleven of my men, we discovered, among a number of intriguing things, a note. This was written on a small piece of paper, and it turned up, not in either of the dead girls' rooms, but in the bedroom originally allocated to Mr. Saul Raven. The note, presently being examined for traces of fingerprints, reads as follows:

'Don't come out. I'll meet you in the empty room.'

Did any of you write that note? Or, do any of you know who wrote that note? Mr. Raven?"

Everyone turned to look at Saul, who didn't seem in the least agitated.

"I've already told you," said the tall blond, while Libby squirmed slightly beside him, "I've never even been in that room."

"No, I thought not. So, another mystery. How many does that make? Let's see. The missing driver. The rock, and the note—given the condition of the note, I suspect that it came in with the rock, so for now we will count them both as a single puzzle. Then there's Ruthie's money. Oh, and I haven't yet mentioned the obvious matter of the gravel."

Though no one in the room flinched at the word "gravel", several of the students, including Saul this time, flushed slightly. The detective no doubt took notice. His manner was maddeningly perplexing. Now, rather than seeming to list the enigmatic features of a tragic situation, the police chief appeared to be showily laying out his trumps. Under the guise of an almost

playful spirit of goodwill and shared confidence, he
suggested, questioned, paused, grinning all along, and
though he had yet to make any outright accusations,
he seemed to be building up to that, which rendered
his silences more nerve-racking and dreadful than any
explicit contention he could have made.

"You see," he continued gently, "every Friday
evening, before he returns home to Camford, the gardener, Mr. Cadwallader, rakes the gravel at the back of
the house. We have confirmed that he did this yesterday, around six-thirty pm. But we found evidence—of
an unspecific but irrefutable sort—that several people trod over that gravel between last night and this
morning, and this despite claims that no one left the
house after dinner. If you all remained inside, we must
assume that several people visited the house during
the night, though whether or not they were invited
inside has yet to be made clear. And with regard to
this same matter of visitors, my officers have gone
as far as the dilapidated little church, located at no
inconsiderable distance from the back gardens, and
found thereabout traces of recent human activity."

Saul Raven seemed to breathe more easily at this
latest information, as did one or two of the other students, and Hiawatha and Antigone could see that
Detective Greene was producing these pieces of evidence in order to keep them off balance, to provoke

them and then to relieve them, to force them to give something away, if only, at this stage, by a slight shift in posture or the emission of a little sigh or gasp. His tactics were quite effective, because by now it was obvious that most of the people present did have something to say, and yet, no one was the least bit forthcoming. They seemed in fact like a gang of children playing blindman's buff; when Greene came too close with his groping insinuations, they backed silently away. They were too innocent or inexperienced to realize that the police chief could see through his blindfold, and that, in retreating, they were already acknowledging something significant. What, Antigone wondered, were they all hiding? She communicated this question with a look in the direction of her brother, who responded in kind, his eloquent expression a reminder to Tig that all college-age students have secrets—some romantic, some dirty, some unpleasant, most merely private—and in keeping them lies one of the primary joys of youth.

"Now," continued the detective, for the first time betraying impatience, "I have read all of the statements, and I find that each of you claims to have been in bed asleep long before two o'clock this morning. Would anyone care at this time to elaborate as to exactly WHERE you were asleep, or in WHOSE bed, if not your own?"

Several of the students stared at Paula, as though the inspector had directed this inquiry to her alone. But Greene's strategy was not so predictable. He swung around suddenly (an action the swiftness of which, especially after the meal he had just eaten, seemed hardly to be expected of such a mountain of flesh), and, gazing intently into the face of Michael Teller, roared out.

"You, Mr. Teller! Can you tell me what time your roommate, Mr. Augustus, came to bed?"

Now everybody squirmed, including Antigone. She realized, as did most of the other people in the room, that the police chief was going to conquer by dividing them. They would not speak for themselves, so he would force them to speak about each other. Michael Teller, as was his wont, ducked his head, just in case the detective had launched something more tangible than a question in his direction. When no missile whizzed by, Michael raised his head again, and stammered a reply.

"Well, I can't say exactly. Because, . . . because . . ."

"Yes?" insisted Greene, rather ferociously.

"Because I was in the library! Asleep. I fell asleep in the library."

Lady Elevenish, who had probably not visited her own library more than once in the past five years, laughed out loud at the poor student's confession. Really it was more like a hoot. Then she spoke out.

"Well, Detective Greene. Clearly it's the little bookworm who killed the girls!"

The inspector turned an angry face upon her, but said nothing. Hiawatha, recognizing again the gap between his own way of handling the world and that of his hostess (in every sense of the word), was at the same time filled with gratitude for her fearlessness and the natural way she assumed control. He considered admiringly, and for the first time, that Lucy Elevenish was a woman who, like most people, was capable of absurdity, but she was also a mistress of the absurd. Nevertheless, the levity she provided was to prove short-lived.

"Yes, Mr. Teller?" said Greene, turning again to the young man. "You're telling us that you spent the entire night in the library?"

"Yes, that's correct," answered Michael, with a bit more confidence, though he was still ready to run if he had to.

"And why didn't you say so to begin with?"

"I don't know. I didn't intend to fall asleep. But it's such an amazing library!" Here Michael nodded to Lady Elevenish his congratulations on her splendid collection of books. She nodded back, aware only of the money they had cost her, a sum of which she was fiercely proud, though she was also secretly unconvinced as to the actual value of what she had gained. The library was Manfred's domain. Michael went on.

"Then, when the murders were discovered, I was afraid that, not having spent the night in my room, I might be a suspect. You see, I've been a suspect before. Once, when I was in kindergarten back home in Missouri, a girl named Marla Grabb lost her ring, and the teacher, Miss Wark, made us all stay after school till it was found, and she—Miss Wark—kept looking at me, because, it's true, I had taken an interest in the ring, and had asked to see it, but only to confirm that the stone was a fake. She—the teacher—even asked me straight out and in front of everyone when was the last time I had seen it; I said it had been days before, but I don't think she believed me. They never did find it, as far as I know."

Thus Michael Teller disburdened himself of what was presumably his earliest experience in the role of the wrongly accused. The others marveled at his strange volubility; some were tempted to laugh, but Hiawatha empathized with Michael's paranoia, and Antigone was sympathetic, no doubt because the young man reminded her of her brother. Michael might have gone on to recount other memories of similar misjudgments had not Detective Greene intervened.

"Yes, riveting," he said, with unmasked sarcasm. "And about your night in the library, which is after all not far from the rear entrance of the house. Did you hear or see anything unusual?"

"Well," Teller was now subdued. "I thought I heard some noises outside, and some people talking and laughing, but I was awfully tired, and I can't be sure it wasn't my imagination. Anyway, it certainly wasn't the sound of people killing each other." He frowned, and was relieved that he had finally said all he could on the topic. Greene made a sort of low grunt before continuing.

"And so you, Mr. Augustus, have no witness that you were in your room all night. Tell me, were you, too, irresistibly drawn to the cases of incunabula in Lady Elevenish's private *bibliothèque*? Or do you still maintain that you remained all night in the bed to which you were originally assigned?"

Rupert glared around him like a trapped lion. Then he answered in a surly tone.

"Well, I did leave my room once, for a few minutes. I was looking for —"

As Rupert was speaking, slowly, as though to put off a revelation he was unsure he wanted to make, Paula Simon stood up abruptly. She seemed like a Puritan borne under an accumulation of stones during a trial for sorcery. When she opened her mouth, the sound was the unmistakable wail of one whose mental resolve has been broken by physical means.

"I know what you're all thinking! That I was sharing a room with Kimberly Ann, so I must have killed her, thinking she was Ruthie! But it wasn't me!" She screamed. "I never left my bed the whole night."

With that, and leaving the others in visible turmoil, Paula Simon fled the room. Lady Elevenish looked poisonously toward the inspector, who immediately instructed Tony and Hiawatha not to go after Miss Simon, but to let her alone, for now. Then the detective sat quietly for a moment, as though deep in meditation, his own heavy breath a kind of incense carrying his secret prayers up to the plaster deities embossed on the lofty ceiling. Hiawatha returned to his seat, wheezing slightly and feeling feverish again. Antigone looked more thoughtful than astonished; the others, including Mrs. Shant and the two maids, were quite pale, but also fascinated by the exciting turn of events. Finally, in a corner of the room, Feathers remained silent and motionless—in a word, unruffled.

X

BREAD OF WAR

(Being a mistranslation of the actual dessert)

TELL ME EVERYTHING YOU SAW WHEN YOU CAME INTO the room. Ruthie's room, I mean."

Antigone was sitting in one of the two comfortable chairs before the window in her bedroom. She was wearing a light flannel nightgown, and her eyes were glowing with interest. Hiawatha, buttoned up in long pyjamas and wrapped in a Scottish blanket, sat opposite his sister, half-listening to her and half-listening for footsteps that might warn him of Lady Elevenish's approach, which he dreaded and desired in exactly equal measure.

It had been a relief to everyone when, a few minutes after Paula Simon's outburst and her subsequent flight from the Chinese sitting room, Inspector Greene had adjourned the informational meeting, reminding them all as they departed that they would reconvene the next day at lunchtime. So it was now official, the planned two-day weekend at Lostlindens was to be prolonged indefinitely. The decision was greeted with a range of emotions from delight to worry by the students, a vague fear of professional repercussions by both Hi and Tony, and silent but prodigious irritation by Lady Elevenish, who still dreamed of having her house empty again except for the nightly visits of Hiawatha. As though she had gotten the idea from the mysterious note found in Saul Raven's room, Lucy had hastily scribbled a message for Hiawatha on a little piece of paper, promising to come and find him later in the evening; this she passed him discreetly as they left the presence of Inspector Greene. Hence Hi's relief that his sister had not only not been too tired to talk after the meeting, but had actually insisted that her brother come to explain and clarify certain details of the morning's discoveries while they were still fresh in his mind. So he had changed out of his clothes in record time and was now folded up neatly under the blanket, sniffing at regular intervals, his attention heightened, but also divided, as we have seen.

"What I remember," Hi began distractedly, and in a staccato whisper, as though to set an example for his sister to follow, "is the horrid look on her face. 'Agape' is the word that comes to mind. Not only her mouth, but her nose and her eyes. Her eyes were the worst of all. Think of Munch's *Scream*, and multiply it by ten."

"Yes, but what about her surroundings? Was there any sign of a struggle, anything broken? Anything at all out of the ordinary?

"Oh Tig, who can say what was ordinary for Ruthie Slatt? If she'd slept naked with a string of sausages around her neck and an axe under her pillow, it would hardly have been a surprise. Poor thing. But of course, you mean seriously. Let me see. Except for her head, she was under the covers. The room was dark, curtains drawn, lights off. Her rucksack hanging by a strap from a chair between the windows. Now that I think of it, there was something on the nightstand next to the bed. It was a piece of candy, shaped like a little fruit—maybe more than one. You see, on the dinner table last night was a sort of elaborate silver serving dish, with arms like a tarantula, and at the end of each was a little pile of chocolates and sugared chestnuts and—oh, you know, miniature painted fruits, what are they called?"

"Marzipan?" Tig suggested.

"That's it! I may not know the name, but I knew I liked them—you recall I'm a fanatic for almond paste—so I was horrified to find they were just out of my reach. But Ruthie was right in front of them. When we found her body, I definitely noticed at least one on her bedside table, because I remember thinking that it would have been just like Ruthie to have snatched some and taken them away up her sleeve, even hustled out of the room as she had been in the violent circumstances which marked the end of the meal."

"Interesting," intoned Tig, deep in thought. "I wonder if we could get into that room to have a look at the table. I don't suppose Mr. Greene will share what they've found, but I might be able to make something of it, if there's some powder or something."

"But I saw several of the students eating those little fruit things, and none of them died. I guess you're suggesting that, if she was poisoned, that may have been the vehicle, someone having, shall we say, intervened with the . . . pandemars?"

"Marzipan. Yes. They'd be perfect for poison, the texture pliable, the surface granular." Tig was becoming analytical, or rather, resuming her natural analytical approach to the world, which she had set aside in the initial excitement of rushing over to England and reuniting with her distinctly non-analytical brother.

"Well we certainly can't get into the room now. There's a policeman stationed in the corridor, and has been continuously since this morning. Makes me feel like we're stuck in the Tower of London, awaiting trial."

"Yes, your situation is rather like that of Ann Boleyn, with Lady Elevenish as King Henry VIII, brooking no treason or escape. But tell me, was Ruthie on any medications? Did she have any health problems that you know of?"

"Well, I've given the student health forms, which are always brought along on these study programs, to the police. But naturally I had a good look at them before I did." Hiawatha may not have been as analytical or systematic as his sister, but he was quick-thinking, and his curiosity more than matched her own. "According to what she stated on her form, she suffered from practically every ailment known to favor a student population. Let me see, she was mildly dyslexic, had Attention Deficit Disorder, was borderline manic-depressive, hyperactive, had 'anger issues'—I can vouch for that—God knows what else. Boils, hangnails, infected piercings and, though it wasn't listed, probably an allergy to marzipan. Poor thing."

"And did she take prescription medications?"

"Well, surprisingly, for all of this, she only took an anti-depressant. I remember the form said something like 'Verulam' and in parentheses, 'generic Prozac'. To me it sounded more like a truth serum than a real drug. And she certainly did speak her mind on every topic."

Hiawatha was just about to describe several instances illustrative of Ruthie's openness, her already legendary and consistently overwhelming willingness to say whatever came into her head, when there was a light tap at Antigone's door. Hiawatha nearly hit the roof. Throwing his blanket over the chair, he ran toward the closet on the other side of the room.

"It's Lady Elevenish!" he whispered loudly. "I'll just get in here. Tell her I've gone to bed."

Allowing his sister no time to argue, Hi disappeared into the closet. Antigone opened the bedroom door, but the person she found outside was not Lucy Elevenish, it was Paula Simon. The young woman fairly fell into the room.

"Oh Miss Musing. I mean, Professor Musing."

"Call me Antigone," said Tig calmly, making way for Paula to come in, and closing the door after her.

Hiawatha, stuck now, but only in the sense of being pinned, like Polonius behind the arras in Queen Gertrude's bedroom, opened the closet door a crack, in order to hear what transpired. He heard his sister offer Paula a seat, which the other accepted readily. Then, after a sort of natural hush like that preceding the rise of the curtain at a theatrical performance, Paula dissolved in tears.

"Oh Antigone," she sobbed. "I'm in trouble. And since you're Professor Musing's sister, I thought maybe I could talk to you. And you're a woman, so you will understand. And Molly Version told me that you were married to a much older man."

Tig blinked at this, but Paula went on without a pause.

"And you're new here, so you won't be prejudiced by what the others might think. I've got to tell someone my problem, or else I'll go out of my mind."

Antigone's reaction to this show of emotion, and Paula's unquestioning trust in her, was many-sided. She was touched, but also rather daunted by what appeared to be the direness of the girl's dilemma. And of course, above all, she was curious as to what she had to tell.

"Well, Paula, you can say whatever you like to me, in confidence," here Tig eyed the closet, all at once bemused by, ashamed of, and grateful for her brother's unseen presence. "And I will give you whatever help I can. But I should tell you in advance that whatever you have to confess, you will also be wise to share with the police."

Paula's crying redoubled in force. Tig, who was standing in front of her, placed a hand gently on her shoulder and waited for the wave of sadness to subside. After a moment there was a lull, and then Paula spoke again, with a little more composure.

"The situation is this. Of course I wasn't in my own bed the night that Ruthie and Kimberly Ann were killed. Everybody knows that. I myself almost died when I discovered Kimberly Ann's body in the other bed the next morning. But I'm jumping ahead. You see," and here she indulged in another discharge of tears, "you see, I was in Tony's room. Tony—that is, Dr. Trefthven-Woooser. We've become very close, and I'm terrified I may be getting him into trouble. We've spent a lot of time together." Here she stared insistently at Tig, in order to pinpoint, without verbalizing, the precise nature of her relationship with the pedigreed English don. "So anyway, when I came to his room—as I had been doing in London for some time—he wasn't there. So I thought to myself, 'Well of course he'll be back shortly.' So I undressed and climbed into bed, as a kind of surprise. I've done it before," she added, in a distinctly defensive and proprietary tone, which Tig recognized as that of a woman entering the stage of love when she is consolidating her holdings. "But," and here she faltered, "he never came." And then she started crying all over again.

Tig was absorbed in Paula Simon's story, though it was hardly her first brush with the notion of student-teacher romance. Paula whimpered for a few more moments, and then asked, in quite a different tone from her confession up to now, "Do you think he's mad at me? Or is it simply that he's nervous about being with a student?"

Tig was rather alarmed, as was her brother in the closet, by this disjunction in Paula Simon's narrative. Suddenly she was not a terrified young woman, compromised by her shadowy behavior during and after a double murder. Suddenly she was a weary housewife desperate for advice on how to facilitate her affair with the milkman. Tig tried to respond in such a way as to reassure her, but at the same time lead her back to stating the facts of the case from her—in one sense anyway—privileged perspective.

"I'm sure Mr. Trefthven-Woooser is trying to do the right thing for both of you. At least I hope so. But you waited for him the entire night? And then what happened?"

"Oh, I finally fell asleep," replied Paula morosely.

"You didn't leave the room? You didn't go looking for him?"

"Well, I was about to. I thought perhaps he was in Saul Raven's room, because everyone knew that either Saul's or Libby's room would be empty." At this, Paula's lips pursed prudishly, and she rolled her eyes. Like a surprising number of people, her own sexual escapades rendered her no less censorious of others indulging in similar activities.

"But when I opened the bedroom door to leave, there was Rupert Augustus, staring down the corridor at me. It was like he was waiting for me! He's so evil! I was sure he was about to tell everyone where I was at that horrible meeting this evening. That's why I had to run away. It was for Tony's sake more than my own."

While Paula was unquestionably sincere when she made this claim, it was obvious to Antigone that at this point, Tony's and Paula's "sakes" were one in the same entity, at least in the latter's mind.

"Anyway, I'm sure he saw me. So I closed the door again quickly." Paula was now dry-eyed and proceeding calmly with her story. "Then I guess I just fell asleep. It looks like the same thing happened to Michael in the library. You know we've all been working very hard, and we're tired most of the time. And when I woke up the next morning, I raced into my own room and quickly changed clothes, and never even noticed that it wasn't Ruthie asleep in the other bed."

Hiawatha in his hiding place could not help but ponder the irony of Kimberly Ann's having been mistaken for Ruthie Slatt, something which would have irritated the self-styled southern belle no end. He unwillingly pictured her in the morgue, wincing at Paula Simon's words.

"Now what should I do?" asked Paula, after another pause. It looked as though she was about to start crying all over again. Tig wanted to head that off, so she spoke decisively.

"Well the first thing you're going to do is to get a good night's sleep."

Paula seemed rather disappointed by this counsel, which would put an abrupt period to what she had planned as a wonderfully self-soothing divagation on the subject of her affair with an attractive and established scholar, single and in possession of a distinguished, double-barreled name. Like so many college English majors, Paula pictured herself as the composite of all of her favorite characters from romantic fiction: she had long curling hair, just like Cathy in *Wuthering Heights*; she was not rich, but neither was Isabel Archer in *The Portrait of a Lady*—at least not to begin with; moreover Paula's own father had once been involved in a lengthy, ruinous lawsuit, just like Maggie's in *The Mill on the Floss*. To be told by Professor Musing—after all, only seven or eight years older than herself—to go to bed at the very moment of crisis in her personal affairs, was like having a cup of cold water splashed on the still-wet ink of the manuscript of her life, a life which, anybody could foresee, was to prove a culminating achievement in the history of heroic female characterizations. Nevertheless, she could hardly refuse the older woman's advice, though she did hesitate.

"Yes, but what should I do? Should I tell the police everything?"

It seemed to Tig that Paula Simon was weighing in her mind at this moment, not so much the danger to which she might be exposing her lover if she were to disclose their affair, but whether or not the disclosure would force the hand—in some way that Tig could not confidently extrapolate—of Tony Trefthven-Woooser. After all, this would not be the first time a faculty member had engaged in a sexual relationship with a student, and no doubt Paula realized that too. Did she want to marry him? For her part, Antigone was less inclined to think that marriage was in the cards, given what appeared to be Tony's recent and rather pointed avoidance of the young woman. All of which was frankly outside the pale of Tig's interest in the deaths of the two girls.

"Well Paula," Tig responded thoughtfully, though her thoughts were tending toward other concerns, "I think you must tell the police where you spent last night. In that way you are being honest, and since Doctor Trefthven-Woooser was not with you, as the police already know, you won't, as far as I can see, be doing him any harm." And saying this, Tig squeezed Paula's arm in a friendly gesture which indicated that it was time for them to part. Paula stood up, still a tiny bit reluctant to end so compelling a conversation on what was, for her, the most fascinating topic—herself. But in the end, she opted to return to the single bedroom to which she had been newly assigned, in case Tony might come looking for her. She shook Antigone's hand warmly and exited the room with the strangely vestal air of one ever-ready to sacrifice herself to a higher purpose.

When, almost simultaneously with Paula's departure, Hiawatha extracted himself from the closet, he immediately blew his nose, having refrained from such an action for the duration of Paula's stay. Then he and his sister exchanged long, meaningful looks, before either of them spoke.

"Well. I hardly know what to think. It's pretty bad for Tony, if in fact he's messing around with a student. It puts my own vague relationship with Lady Lucy quite in the shade." Hi said this musingly and not maliciously, seating himself on the edge of his chair as though he did not plan to stay.

"Yes, the girl's quite worked up. But it doesn't explain anything about the murder of Ruthie or Kimberly Ann. Except of course it helps us to understand why nobody heard anything when Kimberly Ann was killed. Paula wasn't in the room, and next door, both

Rupert and that poor kid, the one Lady Elevenish called the 'little bookworm' —"

"Michael Teller."

"Yes, the one who reminds me a bit of you. They were both gone. And, speaking of bookworms, do you remember when you used to read?"

Hi frowned at this playful, tangential jab. His dwindling commitment to scholarly research could not be denied, at least not to someone as perceptive as his sister. He therefore made no attempt to defend himself, but waited for his sister to go on.

"Anyway," said Tig, "there's still the probability that Libby's room, on the other side of Paula's and Kimberly Ann's, was empty as well. We'll have to find out about that."

"I'll tell you what. You should get some sleep, Tig. And so should I, if I don't want to lose a lung. So why don't I just go back to my bedroom, and on the way, I'll stop at Libby's room—where I'm sure to find Libby and Saul—and ask them what's what."

Tig was a bit surprised at her brother's sudden and uncharacteristic initiative, especially as his proposal would force him to negotiate the corridors alone. The truth was, after hearing Paula's story, and learning that his colleague was having an affair with a student, Hiawatha felt slightly less afraid of encountering Lady Elevenish. As it was nearly eleven o'clock, and they were indeed both tired, Antigone approved his plan, and Hiawatha, saying good-night, slipped out into the hall.

Once on his own, Hiawatha's resolve flagged somewhat. Nevertheless, he walked directly past his own bedroom and stopped outside the door with Libby Moss's name on it. He had already knocked when he realized that he was wearing only his pyjamas and his old bathrobe, but then, they had all seen each other in their night clothes over the past three weeks, and besides, it was too late to run and get dressed now. After a moment, Libby opened the door.

"Yes?" said the willowy blonde, wearing a long tee shirt like a nightgown, with the words "DEATH IS ALL—International Goth Night 2002" printed in bold black letters on the front. Libby herself seemed an unlikely vehicle for such a message, her pretty, placid face with its large blue eyes, like her tall, slender frame, conveying the contradictory idea that life, when thus embodied, was at least *something*.

"Oh it's you, Professor Musing. Come in," said Libby.

Hiawatha entered the room. On the bed, in a pair of boxer shorts and a tee shirt that was identical to Libby's, Saul Raven stretched out, his head propped up by numerous pillows.

"Yeah, come on in, Professor Musing," said the invariably unabashed Saul. "We've been wanting to talk to you, but we weren't sure how."

"Well," Hiawatha began as usual, considering now that he could just as easily have waited till morning to confront the students on the topic of their whereabouts the previous night. Still, he was not uncomfortable speaking to them. Their excessively public love-making notwithstanding, Saul and Libby were among Hi's favorite pupils—both had taken classes with him their freshman year—and he knew them to be intelligent and basically mature; he even envied the calm assurance with which, like a two-person committee that had never known dissension, they coolly faced and in effect outnumbered the world they had already discovered to be made up almost exclusively of individuals, strengthened as they were by their consistent unanimity.

"Talk to me now," said Hiawatha casually. Meanwhile, he found himself once again listening for sounds in the corridor.

"There's not too much to tell," said Saul, exchanging a nod with Libby. Saul was the usual spokesperson for the pair. "It's just that Libby and I didn't spend the entire time here last night, as we led the police to believe. You see, yesterday was Libby's birthday —"

"I'm twenty," interjected Libby.

"Happy Birthday, Libby," said Hi. What else could he say?

"So we wanted to do something wild. I had this idea. Around midnight, we sneaked out the big entrance at the back of the house. We went out to one of the greenhouses and let ourselves in. We had a picnic with stuff we'd saved from dinner. That nice cook gave us an opened bottle of wine when we went up to bed—we'd told her it was Libby's birthday."

"Then this morning," interrupted Libby, "when the bodies were found, we panicked and decided to keep it a secret."

"But when the big police dude said there were 'signs of activity in the gravel'—" here Saul did an admirable imitation of Superintendent Greene, "we knew we'd have to tell the truth. Not that we'd ever really lied. I mean we did come back to bed, but not till five."

Hiawatha was by no means curious as to the details of the five-hour picnic. He looked at the two of them and waited to see if they had anything else to say. Saul shifted his weight slightly, before beginning again.

"But I know we weren't the only ones moving over the gravel, because we heard more than one person while we were out there, though we didn't see anyone. And besides, Detective Greene said that somebody—maybe more than one person—went all the way to the old chapel. But Libby and I never went anywhere near there."

"It's true," agreed Libby, unnecessarily, for the very idea that the two students would disagree on anything was impossible to imagine. Hiawatha wondered if he had ever in his life known, even for a moment, the kind of complete accord with another that Saul and Libby lived in as their primary element, the tandem existence that to Hi seemed utterly unthinkable, not to mention, hardly desirable. Nor did he think this could really be love, the concept of prolonged togetherness being, for Hi, at odds with nature. Consequently he never ceased to be impressed by the anomaly of these young people.

As Saul and Libby had apparently disburdened themselves of all that was weighing on their minds, and as Hiawatha was suddenly more intrigued with questions concerning the nature of love, the latter turned to leave. Before saying good-night, Hi thanked them both, and told them that they should have no worry about sharing the information with Inspector Greene. Not that Libby and Saul were prone to worry, armed as they always were with one another.

Stepping from the room, Hiawatha looked down the long corridor in either direction.

At one end sat a policeman in uniform, who nodded his head at Hi. And hastening toward him from the opposite end, swathed in a rich mantle of silk the color of the Roman sky on a summer night, was Lady Elevenish. She paid absolutely no attention to the constable at the end of the hall. In fact, she looked distracted—perhaps she had been looking for her young professor for some time, though he was not so egotistical as to jump to this conclusion. Furthermore her lips were moving, as though she was already engaged in a conversation with herself or an invisible companion. When she reached Hiawatha, the first thing she said seemed to be another in an ongoing series of declarations.

"And I've thought about it, my dear," she spoke in a low voice, taking him by the arm, "and I've decided that you must be the librettist of the tragicomic opera that is my life."

Uh oh, thought Hiawatha, feeling suddenly like William Holden in *Sunset Boulevard*. But when he turned to Lucy, he could see, despite the perfect and no doubt recent arrangement of her hair and face, that she was upset about something, possibly even on the verge of tears. And it was by no means merely pity for her loneliness that made Hiawatha return with her down the labyrinth of lovely corridors to her room.

XI

GETTING TO KNOW THE STUDENTS

(Or at least some of them, to some extent)

I ASKED TO SEE YOU, PROFESSOR MUSING. RUTHIE spoke so highly of you. She wrote home just about every other day, and she mentioned you all the time. Why, I wouldn't be surprised if she had a girlish crush on you! Said you seemed to think pretty well of her, too. A bit of a teacher's pet, I suppose. She certainly was my little pet."

Hiawatha was utterly perplexed at hearing this news, and only just barely able to keep from betraying the one or two less noble of the many mixed emotions which such information aroused in him.

It was ten o'clock in the morning. Hi was sitting in the Lostlindens library, in an ancient armchair the joints of which seemed very loose, so that every slight shift of his body resulted in the most ominous crepitations. Across from Hi, separated from him by a great sixteenth-century stone fireplace piled inside with unlit logs, stood a tall man in a dark blue suit and a darker blue tie. His hair was graying at the temples, his face lined, especially around the eyes, but otherwise he presented the exterior of a robust and relatively attractive, middle-aged, professional man. This was William Slatt, Ruthie's father, who had arrived only hours ago from Chicago. After a pause, during which Mr. Slatt seemed to be struggling against a familiar force that threatened to undermine the quiet masculinity which was the predominant characteristic he projected, he spoke again.

"Mrs. Slatt can't bring herself to come here. I've left her back at the Bothwick Arms. She had her breakfast in bed. Taking it awful badly. Of course, I understand, she's Ruthie's mother and all. But sometimes I don't think women have any idea of the bond that connects a father and a daughter. Not that Ruthie wasn't close to Francine—they had the occasional tiff, to be sure, but they always made up afterward. Still, I think I knew my little girl better than anyone."

Hiawatha remained silent, as though mesmerized by the novel and hardly comprehensible references to Ruthie Slatt as a "pet" and a "little girl." But clearly she had earned, if only by being born, both those and other endearments from the members of her immediate family. Nor was Hiawatha in a position to render judgment as to who had loved Ruthie better, Bill or Francine. Finally he ventured what he considered an innocuous question.

"Did Ruthie have any brothers or sisters?"

"Three of each," said Mr. Slatt proudly, then adding, in a heartbreaking voice, "Ruthie was the oldest, and the others all looked up to her."

Hiawatha tried to picture the six Slatt siblings, like Ruthies of both genders in every size—small, medium, and large—copies of the prototypical, commercial display model that was Ruthie herself. But he could not or dared not concentrate on such an image. Instead, he attempted to console the man as best he could.

"Well, Mr. Slatt —"

"Call me Bill."

"Well, Bill, let me say again how terribly sorry I am that this has happened. I for one shall miss Ruthie's sense of humor, her spark, her energy, her vivid and engrossing way of telling a story. And if there's anything I can do to alleviate your own or your family's suffering, please let me know."

"Actually, you can help me out a bit. I've already talked to that pompous Inspector Greene, and he

seems, like everyone else I've had to deal with in this
country, very tight-lipped. Won't tell me anything I
want to know. Such as what, exactly, killed Ruthie.
He says she was poisoned, but they don't yet know
how. And tell me honestly, do you think it could have
been one of the other students? This Kimmie Ann
Crustview, for example? But she's dead, too. And
Ruthie's always been such a popular girl!"

Confronted with this last notion, Hiawatha was at
a loss for words. He asked himself what Tig would say
in this uncomfortable situation, seated face-to-face
with the father of one of his two (two!) dead students.
He regretted now that his cold had become so much
better, he could no longer take refuge in sneezing or
blowing his nose. Thankfully, Bill Slatt was happy to
continue without a response from Hi.

"I'll tell you something, though," he resumed, in
a decidedly angry tone, "if they won't play ball with
me, I'll be just as difficult with them. They won't find
out anything about Ruthie until they show me their
cards."

Hiawatha was about to question the wisdom of
holding back anything that might help the police to
find Ruthie's killer, if in fact she had been killed, for
the possibility of suicide had not yet been ruled out.
But before Hi could open his mouth, Mr. Slatt produced a loud and wrenching lament.

"Oh I always knew something like this might happen!!"

While the man's despair nearly moved Hiawatha to tears, he could not help being struck by the coincidence that linked Mr. Slatt, in his expression of a retroactive expectation that his daughter might die in unnatural circumstances, with Mrs. Miranda Crestview Frink, who had made much the same remark about her own daughter to Antigone. And slowly an idea dawned upon Hi.

"Mr. Slatt—I mean, Bill. Do you mind if I ask what you do for a living?"

Bill Slatt left off his lamenting as abruptly as he had taken it up. In fact, there was a gleam in his eye, and Hi took this to signify that his question had been a very apt and intelligent one.

"I take your point, Professor Musing —"

"Call me Hiawatha."

Bill Slatt made a face as though to say that he could never call anyone by such a name. Then he went on.

"You see, I can tell you're ten times smarter than that fat police detective. He never asked me anything important—in fact, he was clearly trying to put me off."

Hi waited silently for the answer to his inquiry into Mr. Slatt's occupation. He had just remembered the stories Ruthie was telling the night before she died, about her father's closeness to the criminal world back in Chicago. Perhaps, after all, these murders were minor moves in a much larger underworld game, the playing field of which stretched considerably farther than the graveled walk behind Lostlindens. Sweat broke out on Hiawatha's brow, as it had done hours earlier in Lady Lucy's arms, but for very different reasons. He waited in suspense for Mr. Slatt, who, for the briefest moment, seemed to resemble a slick-suited Midwestern gunman from the prohibition era, to confess that he was himself a notorious criminal. In fact, the man was quite the opposite, as Hi was relieved to hear.

"My occupation? I am the director and chief warden of the Federal Penitentiary in Elkhart, Indiana. With over eight-thousand inmates, the largest federal prison in the United States."

"I see!" said Hi, voluminously exhaling. *Thank God*, he thought to himself. "And so you thought something like this might have happened to Ruthie because of some sort of convict's revenge? Is that what you meant a moment ago?"

"Exactly," said Mr. Slatt, appreciating Hiawatha's quick deduction and never suspecting him of any other. "And now, I'll confide in you something I haven't yet had a chance to tell the stuffy English police. The bus driver who brought you here? Mr. MacMenzies? He was one of my men."

In spite of his efforts to hide it from the speaker, Hiawatha was altogether befuddled by this incongruous declaration.

"What do you mean?"

"Just what I said. He was a prisoner in Elkhart several years ago. That's right, we get 'em from all over the world. Why I've had every kind, from kingpins of the Russian Mafia to Peruvian kidnappers, in my jail. This man, Bertie MacMenzies, was a Scot who came to our country years ago as a teenage tourist. He wrote bad checks in every state of the Union. Probably killed a couple of people, too, though they never proved that. Finally got him on a mail fraud charge. When his sentence was over and he was released, I helped him find decent work as a driver. And then when Ruthie begged to go on this study abroad thing, well, I was worried about her . . ."

"Worried about her?" Hi wondered aloud.

"Well, you can imagine. A little Midwestern girl all alone. And you see, in my job, you often hear threats from disgruntled mobsters and the like, about getting you back one way or another for keeping them locked up. You know what I mean. 'Keep an eye on your wife and kids, Mister.' That sort of thing. It's a helluva way to live."

"So you arranged for this man to become our bus driver?" Hiawatha could not help being impressed. "But how did you do that?"

Mr. Slatt, now appearing to Hi as a very clever
man, was a bit cryptic.

"Let's just say I've got connections."

"Oh, you mean friends in high places?"

"Well, in fact, friends in low places. But that's neither here nor there."

Hiawatha was trying to digest these latest revelations. With regard to MacMenzies, he was stupefied,
though, come to think of it, he had initially found the
driver rather strange, and even a little seedy. After
all, what Scot still living on this side of the Atlantic
would listen endlessly to bagpipe music on the radio?
No, that was either pent-up nostalgia, or else he was
doing his best to *seem* Scottish, possibly both. And
Ruthie, who had asked for MacMenzies' whereabouts
at the end of her last meal—no doubt she was puzzled
by the absence of her private bodyguard. It was all
more than interesting enough to make Hiawatha desperate to find his sister and tell her everything he had
learned.

"But didn't the police tell you? Mr. MacMenzies
has disappeared."

Mr. Slatt smiled vaguely when Hiawatha said
this.

"Bertie's a tough man to predict. He could be anywhere. But should I tell you what I think?" Slatt's
voice, from which the tender sadness of his earlier

intimations had now drained away, was becoming increasingly cold. He stared at Hiawatha for a considerable period, without really registering his presence. At last Hi broke into the lull.

"Yes, please do tell me what you think," said the English professor, nervously.

The warden stood up slowly, as though about to leave. Instead, he walked over to Hiawatha's chair. Resting his hands on the unstable arms and holding his face very close to the younger man's, Mr. Slatt spoke in a whisper at once calm and chilling.

"I think Bertie MacMenzies knows who killed my daughter, and he's gone to take care of things. I pity the person who did it if Bertie finds him. In prison, he was a legend for his temper."

Bill Slatt stood up, the remote smile never leaving his face, and extended his hand to Hiawatha. Hi shook it automatically, without rising. After Mr. Slatt had exited the library, Hi shuddered, and the spasm made the chair cry out. For a moment he didn't move; in fact, he was mesmerized by his own wild speculations concerning the personal lives of the other students. Just how many of them had connections to the criminal world?—for, as Mr. Slatt had just made frighteningly clear, the world of criminal justice and that of violent crime were virtually one and the same, and criss-crossed the entire globe. When at last

Hiawatha's imagination threatened to unhinge him altogether, he jumped out of the chair, and hurried away from the room.

Earlier that morning at breakfast, Lady Elevenish had looked at once haggard and glowing, as only a middle-aged woman who has stayed up all night in the company of a much younger lover can. If she herself had been younger, the students might have supposed she was high. In the midst of a loud and colorful recital of tales from an imaginary girlhood divided between Bond Street shops and an otherwise unbroken series of hunt balls in the Cotswolds, a policeman had entered the room, escorted by Feathers at his most mortician-like. When the uniformed newcomer announced that a Mr. Slatt had been sent by Inspector Greene to talk to Professor Hiawatha Musing, Antigone, who was seated on the other side of Hi from Lady Lucy, shot him an excited look, which intersected with the more anxious gaze of their hostess, who envisioned nothing less dramatic than a duel between the deceased girl's father and the young professor under whose supervision she had died. For her part, Tig would have liked to accompany her brother to the meeting, but as that might well have inhibited the freshly-arrived Mr. Slatt, she held back from making such a suggestion, deciding instead to begin questioning some of the other students on the program, as she and her brother had arranged when they separated the night before.

And so, shortly after Hiawatha left the banqueting saloon to make the acquaintance of poor Ruthie's father, Antigone found herself following Molly Version from the breakfast table up the oak staircase and down the long corridor to the latter's room. There were several reasons for choosing Molly as the first of her interviewees. To begin with, she was the youngest of the students, a fact which allowed Tig to hope that she might be more easily convinced, if not actually more eager, to share her ideas. But she was also, clearly, one of the brightest and most perceptive among them, so that she might have noticed or understood things that had escaped the rest. Finally, Molly was, to judge from outward appearances, by far the least agitated or disarranged by the bizarre incidents that must have affected them all. Tig had observed this, and it had intrigued her, at breakfast, which most of the students had eaten as they had eaten their dinner the night before, rather quickly and in relative silence. A few of them, including Rupert Augustus and Sarah Magister, had begun to grumble, complaining about the disruption in their itinerary and challenging the legality of Inspector Greene's decision to imprison them at Lostlindens for an indefinite period. Michael

Teller had been happy to supply a brief history of the laws of *habeas corpus*, though he couldn't say for certain that they would apply to students held for a few extra days in a magnificent country house which was the scene of a double murder. Throughout this—for the most part mumbled—discussion, Molly, seated as of old between Paul Stripling and Herman Wadkin, had set her face to an extended smirk, at last rising to leave the room alone.

When Tig knocked on Molly's door, Feathers opened it. This surprised Antigone, who had not seen him go in. The butler was uncharacteristically loquacious.

"Yes, M'm. I've just been bringing Miss Version a telephone message from her parents."

For some reason Antigone could not identify, there was a slight awkwardness about the three of them meeting there in Molly Version's room in the middle of the morning. Whatever the cause, each one seemed to feel it. Feathers, after making a little bow with his long upper body, spoke again.

"Well, if that will be all . . ."

The remark, which had seemed to Tig to be rhetorical and addressed to nobody in particular, was nevertheless interpreted personally by Molly, whose consent to the butler's departure was made with a showy and confident air that suggested the dismissal

of a chambermaid by Madame de Maintenon shortly
after the Sun King had installed her at Versailles.
Molly was certainly an interesting character for study.
When Feathers was gone, Tig asked if she might talk
to her for a few minutes. Molly seemed gratified by
the request, smiling and asking her to come in.

"How old do you think he is?" asked Molly pensively, seating herself sideways at the head of her bed.
Tig sat down opposite her on a beautifully uphol-
stered *bergère*.

"How old is who?" asked the bewildered visitor.

"Feathers, of course. The butler." Molly laughed
as though nothing could have been more obvious than
the contents of her own mind at that moment.

"Why, I don't know. Fifty? Perhaps a little younger.
It's hard to say with some men. He may have had that
grey coloring all his life. Why do you ask?"

Molly laughed again, reaching for the cigarettes
on her bedside table.

"Oh, just curious. People interest me. All people.
I won't ask you if you want a cigarette. But do you
mind if I have one?"

Tig didn't mind. She had already passed briefly
through that phase during which the modern
mother-to-be is terrified of second-hand smoke
stunting her unborn child's growth. And after all, it
was Molly's room. Molly lit her cigarette, blew at the

match, then tossed it toward the tole canister which served as a waste basket. The match rebounded off the rim, and landed on the rug. Molly grunted, sprawling across the coverlet in order to retrieve and deposit it in its proper place, all of which Tig watched without comment.

When she had resumed her more or less upright position against a bank of embroidered cushions, Molly spoke.

"I know why you're here of course, Mrs. Vander-lyn."

"Goodness, so formal," smiled Tig. "I actually kept my own name, but it doesn't matter. I told Paula Simon she could call me Antigone, and so can you."

Molly looked thoughtful for a moment, then smiled herself, her green eyes sparkling amid a great puff of smoke.

"If and when I get married," proffered Molly, "I will definitely change my name. It seems such an easy and flattering concession to a man's vanity, and think what you might get in return."

Tig had not been wrong in supposing that a talk with Molly would prove enlightening. Still, she had not come to discuss the finer points of post-marital nomenclature. She dropped her eyes briefly, before attempting a transition to the more important issue at hand.

"Well, fortunately for you, there's plenty of time to think about that. I take it you're not engaged right now? I don't think Ruthie or Kimberly Ann were engaged, were they? Because my brother and I are hoping to find out a little more about them, in order to throw some light on this bizarre situation and to get you all on your way again."

"Yeah, it is getting pretty boring, staying in this house. But I'm in no hurry to go to Camford. I'd much rather be back in London. That's what I'm trying to arrange through my parents. I'd like to drop out of the course—nobody will blame us after everything that's happened—and just go back to London for a couple weeks."

"I agree that you've all been through a lot. That's part of the reason I'm here," Tig tried again to wean the younger woman away from the one topic which clearly obsessed her, her own pleasure. In this particular respect Molly was very much like Paula Simon, perhaps like all young people, though Tig could not honestly accuse herself of that singlemindedness of purpose, even when she was younger. "You see," she pressed on, "I'd like to find out more about Ruthie and Kimberly Ann. Did you know either of them very well?"

Molly seemed to be debating in her mind whether or not to answer this question. Tig was struck by the way she smoked, squinting her eyes slightly as she slowly pulled the cigarette away from her mouth.

"Yeah," replied Molly at last, "I had a class with Kimberly Ann, but it's not as though she was a rival or anything."

Here was an insight into Molly's way of seeing things, as well as another reminder of the youth of the people involved in this case. Tig felt that finally she had a little foothold.

"What class was that?"

"Intro to Biochem," said Molly, utilizing the standard abbreviated form of the college course designation.

"I teach that at Clare," said Antigone. "But isn't that a freshman course? I thought Kimberly Ann was a junior."

Molly grinned, not so much maliciously as to indicate that anybody, and especially a teacher, should be able to guess the significance of a junior taking a class normally reserved for freshmen.

"Well, I think she flunked it during her first year. She told me at one of the meetings before this trip that she had decided, 'after great soul-searching'—that's how she put it—that she would have to give up her chemistry major and go straight into her true vocation, hotel management. But I'm sure she flunked the biochemistry course both times."

"And when you say she wasn't a rival, what do you mean?"

"Well," said Molly, apparently a little exasperated, "I mean, look at her!" Then, seeming suddenly conscious of her own callousness, she added with a blush, "Oh, sorry. You never knew her. And I don't suppose you'll be seeing her now. In the morgue, I mean. Gosh. I just meant to say that she wasn't the kind of woman who had a lot of boyfriends. Herman said she reminded him of Ruthie. It's weird, but he was right."

"Did you know Ruthie at all?" Tig continued her interrogation without a pause.

"Only from this course." Molly was more hesitant in her answer to this question, and Tig felt certain that this was because she didn't want to repeat what must have sounded like the brusqueness of her comments on Kimberly Ann. "She was sort of scary. But I'll tell you something: she was smart, too." As though, in expressing an appreciation of Ruthie's brains, she had indulged in a great display of sympathy which, socially speaking, might even now prove a risk to her own reputation, she added a moment later, in a voice that was more like a sigh, "Of course I didn't really spend much time with her."

Antigone was quiet, considering not so much what Molly had already said, as how she herself could introduce the next question, after all the one in which she was most interested. She moved forward tentatively.

"No, you spend most of your time with Herman and Paul, isn't that true?"

Molly arched her back, but did not outwardly betray any suspicions.

"Yes, we've been very happy, the three of us, all during this course."

This reply, as Antigone had somehow anticipated, rang false, seemed even to have been made sarcastically. Now Tig felt she was on surer ground. Using what she had already learned of Molly's character, she adopted a quiet, confidential tone, appealing to the latter's feminine instincts, at the same time surprising herself at the ease with which she slipped into the role of a cold-blooded investigator.

"And tell me, what are those two really like?"

Molly stubbed out her cigarette rather forcefully in a little porcelain dish by the side of her bed.

"Oh they're great." She smiled her most glittering smile. "And I'm glad you asked me. Because I've been wanting to talk to someone before the police question me again. . ."

Molly made a show of reluctance, which Tig could see at once was feigned.

"What about?"

"About Herman and Paul. You see, they've become two of my best friends in the world. And I don't want to get anyone into trouble. Including myself. It's about where we all were on the night of the murders."

"Yes?" Tig encouraged her, not daring to press any harder.

"Well," said Molly, hemming again. Her show of hesitation was apparently not subject to shortening; she had written this part of the script, and no one was going to cut her lines. "It's just that. . ."

Tig wanted to shake her.

"Well, I told the police that I was in my bed that night. And Herman and Paul said that they didn't see me after dinner. But the fact was, I was in their room for several hours."

Tig was a bit lost.

"But what does it matter if you spent part of the night with your friends? I'm sure the inspector would understand."

"Yes," continued Molly, stretching out the affirmation to three syllables. "But I think that Herman and Paul might be upset if I said what we were doing."

Tig had a pretty good idea of what was to come, but she was unprepared for the sudden impassioned speech, the sheer spate of details that made up Molly's crowning monologue.

"At first we were just talking. Paul had gotten a bottle of wine from somewhere, the kitchen I think. Well, at one point, we all got into bed together. Into Herman's bed. He seemed the least interested to begin with. Paul's been coming on to both of us since the course began. You know, like walking around in his underwear, stuff like that. Pretty childish really. But he always held back from me. I understand that now! Anyway, we all got undressed, and next thing you know, we're all doing it. It was like a scene from a porn film or something. Not that I've seen too many, but you get the idea. And then, after a few minutes of this, you know, sucking and fondling, suddenly Herman and Paul are taking turns on top of one another, and I'm sitting alone at the end of the bed. Can you believe that? I mean, they're gay! I was so pissed."

Tig did not trust herself to vocalize her reaction. If she had, it might have taken the form of some sisterly advice. Bite down hard, she would have said to Molly. Men are sometimes like that.

Molly, out of breath from disburdening herself, smiled once more, a little ferociously. She was even prettier when her pride was damaged. Now, with her green eyes wide and her face slightly flushed, she seemed the very image of Eurydice shipped off to the Underworld while Orpheus entertained the troops— or, to be more accurate with regard to the archetypes of Herman and Paul, while Orpheus played touch football with Hercules.

"Well," said Tig at last, "I don't think Inspector Greene will want to hear all the details of your evening. The important thing is that you tell him where you were."

"But I wouldn't want to keep things from him," said Molly, meekly but again falsely.

She was clearly eager to proclaim the real reason that she had not succeeded in seducing one or both of the best looking men on the course. Tig ignored her pretend scruples.

"The important thing is that you didn't hear or see anything connected to the deaths of Ruthie and Kimberly Ann. I take it that when you left your friends, you didn't notice anything unusual, in the hallway, for example?"

"No. Nothing. After Herman and Paul got all carried away, I just went straight back to my room." Here she paused again, her face slightly curdled in a disingenuous frown. "You know, I really am happy for them, now that I'm used to the idea."

Tig studied that face as she stood up to leave. More like Medea than Eurydice, she thought. Though she was herself no gossip, she was suddenly quite eager to find Hiawatha, to tell him that three more of the living could be accounted for during the period of time that her brother was by now melodramatically referring to as "the night of the dead." She said good-bye to Molly, with a parting smile, leaving the teenager poised, as it seemed, on the brink of what was bound to prove a most fascinating and eventful womanhood.

XII

A FLASHBACK ERASED

*(Wherein the dead walk and talk
and do odd things again)*

HIAWATHA, WHILE REVIEWING THE DETAILS OF HIS conversation with William Slatt, had taken refuge in his sister's bedroom, to await her return from what he correctly assumed must be an interrogation of one of the students. He was forced to acknowledge, if only to himself, that, in avoiding his own room, he was acting on a vague but characteristic inclination to hide. What, precisely, he was hiding from was less clear in his mind. Certainly he was happy to spend a few minutes away from the students and the responsibility they represented, now dramatically increased. They were growing understandably restless. Foreseeing that before long their parents would be expecting news of their welfare, if not their actual return, Hi had spent more than an hour on the telephone the previous afternoon with the president of his college back in Illinois. This man, Dr. Sloan, was a good-hearted septuagenarian humanist, most of whose advice took the form of metaphors drawn from baseball and the social history of the Italian Renaissance. As often as not these metaphors were mixed. So a somewhat mystified Hiawatha had been instructed to rally the team together, to persuade them to be vigilant in the presence of this unseen Borgia assassin, to remember Castiglione's advocacy of honor in the face of aggression, and by no means to bunt. The one fact that had emerged from this discussion was that Hiawatha must maintain a rigorous watch over his charges while continuing to cooperate fully with the English police.

And what of Lady Elevenish? Was he hiding from her as well? Hi pondered the possibility soberly. During the day, it was so difficult to imagine that this wealthy, worldly woman, silly but also kind and clever, was attracted to him. The idea was flattering, though, as Tig knew too, it was also worrisome. Her brother was incapable of relaxing in a sexual relationship. Both were aware that, for Hiawatha, the perfect connections were those that lasted a minute, or at most a little longer. People you bump into, people who smile at you on the bus—these were his truest loves, the only people whose love or even interest he really trusted. An ideal evening would be one in which you were able to perpetuate that kind of feeling—of openness and spontaneous goodwill, of generosity, patience, sympathy, mutual curiosity, and shared delight—for the duration of a meal. But if you actually go home and go to bed with someone, you're already living on borrowed time. Tig could not help but pity her brother, fettered as he was by such notions and such fears. And Hiawatha pitied himself, though the situation made him laugh, too, seeing no immediate solution to what struck most people as his inveterate and perhaps congenital isolation and loneliness.

While Hiawatha was happily indulging in solipsistic reflections such as these, Antigone burst into the room, the abrupt encounter causing them both to jump.

"Thank goodness you're here!" said Tig, flushed and animated.

"Really?" said Hi, with noticeably less spirit than his sister. He was still puzzling over his affair with Lady E.

"How is it, Hi, that you always manage to give the impression that you are merely waiting for the next laundry-bag of bad news?"

Tig sat down across from her brother, and they exchanged detailed summaries of the conversations they had just had, Hi with Bill Slatt, his sister with Molly Version. Tig was dismayed to hear that her brother had not inquired into possible explanations for the large sum of money found in Ruthie's rucksack. The question had altogether slipped Hiawatha's mind. The news of the bus driver, however, more than made up for this lapse, just as Antigone's information about Molly and her misfiring ménage with Herman and Paul came as a complete shock to Hi, putting a period for the time being to his self-absorbed observations on his own love life. Before the siblings had finished expressing their reactions to these latest revelations, there was a loud and urgent knock at the door. Antigone rose to answer it.

"Oh Professor Musing!" said a female voice, and then another, just as frantic as the first, spoke up, "Have you seen your brother?" And then, both in unison, "We've got to talk to him!"

Antigone opened the door further, making way for Mame Freeline and Sarah Magister. The two young women were clearly agitated, talking quickly and seeming, altogether out of character, like two squirrels in a television cartoon. Hiawatha had risen from his chair, so that now he and his sister faced the girls like opponents in a ping-pong match.

"What is it?" said their teacher, dreading, as Tig guessed, some new disaster.

Mame and Sarah glanced briefly at each other, before the latter spoke.

"Well first of all, we've got to tell you something. Something awkward."

"Why don't you both sit down," said Antigone, closing her door again, sensing that another series of confidences was on the way. Rather like an automaton, Sarah sat down in one of the two chairs formerly occupied by Hiawatha and Antigone. Mame, with her handbag over her shoulder, perched on the arm of the same seat. Hi and Tig remained standing.

"The fact is, Professor Musing, Mame has a videotape which includes a few minutes of footage from that horrible dinner—you know—Ruthie's and Kimberly Ann's last meal."

At a nod from Sarah, Mame reached into her bag and brought out the compact tape.

"But you don't mean to say that you filmed that fight?" asked Hiawatha incredulously, though it would have been quite possible for all he had noticed of what the other students were doing during the face-off between Ruthie and Kimberly Ann.

"No, but I filmed the table and everything when we first came down." Mame was speaking now. "I don't think it will be helpful in any way, but before he left the house last night, Inspector Greene asked me if I would be so good as to locate the tape, and produce it for him today. Somebody must have told him I'd been filming things."

"But it's only natural that he would want to have a look at it," said Tig reasonably.

"Yes, we know," agreed Sarah. "The problem is . . ." And here she stopped.

"Problem?" asked Hi, with growing apprehension.

"The problem is that there are one or two things on the tape that might be misconstrued," Mame blurted out. "For example, just before dinner, I was taping Sarah in our bedroom, and there on the bedspread, among our things, is something that someone might mistake for something bad."

Tig decided at this point to sit down in the empty seat. Hi remained standing, confused but even more alarmed. He moved behind his sister's chair, and idly fingered the braided upholstery piping at the top.

"Like what?" he said at last, aiming at nonchalance and distinctly missing his mark.

"Well," Sarah began, but then hesitated, at which point Mame took over again.

"You see, Sarah and I stupidly picked up some pot when we were in London. Just the tiniest little bag. It was a gift from these English guys we met. Honestly, it was no big deal. I was so stupid to film it, but that was an accident. Anyway, when I was rewinding the tape this morning, so that I could give it to the police, I noticed it there. And as the Inspector said that the murders might have involved drugs or something, Sarah and I panicked. We were going to erase it, but then we thought they might somehow be able to tell, and we'd be in real trouble. So we've come to confess to you and to ask for your help."

Though she was clearly sincere in her anxiety, Mame seemed at the same time very much in control, and by no means overly apologetic. As a result, though it went counter to their professional instincts, both Hiawatha and Antigone respected her for her honesty. It was, of course, impossible to condone their use of marijuana, but after teaching for several years, neither Hi nor Tig could muster any intense amazement at the idea of such a crime. In his great confusion—the two women were after all his students, and technically he should discipline them without delay, by informing their parents and, possibly, by immediately suspending them from the course as well—Hiawatha could come up with no clear plan. Before he had said anything, Mame spoke again.

"The funny thing is, we smoked it all that night. It wasn't very good. It made us really hungry."

"Do you mean to suggest," asked Hiawatha, "that you were new to the experience?"

He hoped that if they indicated they were unused to such pleasures, he might risk leniency. At this point, he was ready to destroy the tape himself, as it would only create greater problems for everybody concerned.

"Well," said Sarah, her large eyelashes drooping, "we tried it in London. It was the first time for both of us. Tell him, Mame."

"That's correct. I mean, I have a brother back in Chicago who smokes it all the time, but I was never tempted before. Something about being away from home, I guess."

Hiawatha felt relieved, but was still unsure what to say next, when Antigone jumped in.

"May we see the tape?" she asked.

"Here it is," responded Mame, now very meekly, handing the evidence to Tig.

"Is there some way we can view it? I mean, aside from the little screen on the camera?"

Hiawatha, once again elated that his sister was here to share the moral and psychological dilemmas which continued to spring up around him like mushrooms in a damp wood, nearly shouted out the response that fortuitously came to him.

"Lucy's got a fancy American television set in her bedroom! I'm sure there's a video player. Let's go and ask her to help us. There's still plenty of time before lunch and the dreadful Inspector Greene."

So the four of them set out for Lady Elevenish's rooms at the other end of the house. When they arrived at her door, Hiawatha nearly walked in without knocking; luckily his sister pulled him back just in time, tapping lightly so as not to arouse people in any of the adjoining rooms. Lucy responded to the summons immediately, almost as though she had been listening at her own door.

"Hi!" she rang out into the corridor, seeing her lover had come for her all unbidden, and this was the first time. Then, with slightly less aplomb but not, all in all, a bad show of gratification, she added, "Antigone!" And finally, in a tone which did much, if not quite enough, to dissemble a slight, surprised disappointment, she concluded with, "And others!" She could not remember most of the students' names.

"Lucy," said Hi, excitedly, "we need your help. You see, we've got a tape here, and we want to have a look at it before Mr. Greene insists on carrying it away. You've got a good machine, I think —"

All of a sudden, in the middle of his request, Hiawatha went silent and blushed profusely. Lucy only smiled and seemed not to know how to respond. At this point, Antigone took over.

"You see, Lady Elevenish, Hiawatha thought you might have an American video player that we could use to view this tape, which Sarah and Mame here have been making throughout the course, and which may include something interesting with regard to the current investigation." Then, as if she, too, felt a little of her brother's discomfiture, Antigone continued more formally. "I hope we aren't disturbing you."

"Not at awl," said Lady Elevenish with a laugh, slapping on her own false British manner, which she would not have done with Hiawatha alone, but at this moment the intimate couple were outnumbered. "Come in. I was oonly taking a little nap." Here she could not resist giving Hi a wink.

The five of them now penetrated deeper into Lady Elevenish's private domain, a suite of three elegant, enfiladed rooms which, even to the untrained eye, were instantly recognizable as the most expensively appointed of the smaller chambers in the house. The first of these was actually a sizable salon, the walls richly carved *boiseries* in a slatey grey-green, pierced along one side by six light-filled vertical windows. Beyond, a diminutive sitting or dressing area could be seen, through the open doors of which appeared the bedroom, painted in pink and gold, with, in the center of the far wall, a gorgeous *lit à la polonaise*; this, as Hi had learned from his mistress on their first night together, had once borne the dormant burden of no less a personage than Madame de Pompadour. And at the foot of the venerated bed was a large, state-of-the-art home entertainment center, beyond the wildest dreams of the most techno-dependent American mogul—so large, in fact, that it obliterated most of one wall and actually overlapped the frame of a small pastel attributed to Fragonard.

Sarah and Mame were clearly dazzled by the rooms in which they found themselves, and Hiawatha felt strangely, almost proprietarily, proud. Antigone, on the other hand, had an aversion to the *stil Rothschild*, and consequently did not trust herself to make any remark on the decoration of her surroundings, the overwhelming Frenchness of which came as a surprise from the anglomaniacal Lady Elevenish. The latter, as if reading Tig's mind, explained at once, gradually letting her pronunciational defenses down in the thrill of her reminiscence.

"I pawchased these rooms as a single lote at the Mentmore sale. Awl my friends wanted them—the Bracketts, the Shirkinghams, the Chauncey Waglands. Cost me a bundle, but I got 'em! They're French, of course, which disturbed me at first, but then, they've been in England longer than they were ever in France. Now, about this videotape."

Tig approached the electronic assemblage, with its huge screen and complicated subsidiary appurtenances, like Dorothy before the Wizard of Oz. Lady Lucy relieved her of the tape, and, with admirable know-how in the face of such daunting machinery, inserted it into a larger tape which she took from one of the many shelves. Then, using a remote control appliance, she brought the entire mechanism to life, and stuck the new tape into the video recorder. Immediately the screen was filled with an enormous image of someone's shoe, shot from above.

"That's my foot," explained Mame un-self-consciously. "I sometimes forget to turn off the camera when I'm walking."

"I wonder if we couldn't start at the beginning, and fast-forward through the less important things," suggested Tig, who was delighted at this opportunity to view, as it were, a compact version of the entire course before her arrival. "How much material do you think you have?"

"Oh, a little over an hour, I'd say. I'm halfway through the second tape. I already sent the first one home to my parents," said Mame.

Tig was disappointed that they wouldn't be able to review all the proceedings from the outset.

"The police may ask you to have it sent back," she suggested thoughtfully.

"There wasn't anything—you know—compromising on it, I hope?" asked Hiawatha. He was still worried about how to handle the confession concerning the marijuana.

Sarah and Mame looked at each other for a brief moment, then the former replied calmly.

"There couldn't have been. Really."

While this exchange was taking place, Lady Elevenish was rewinding the tape. When that was finished, she pushed the play button, and what followed was a series of disjointed vignettes, complete with a soundtrack which included a great deal of wisecracking, mainly from off-camera, the voices identifiable as those of the more vocal students, among whom Herman, Molly, and Mame herself were most frequently to be heard. The voice of Ruthie Slatt was also a prominent and, under the circumstances, rather poignant but unsettling reminder of her own presence on the course. Now, thanks to the magic of videography, the people gathered in Lady Elevenish's theatrical bedroom were able to witness, as though conjured up for an encore performance from beyond the grave, Ruthie Slatt at The British Museum, kicking the concrete base upon which rested the Rosetta Stone, and arguing that it was probably a fake. This scene was followed without transition by a lengthy montage of the entire group viewing the Elgin Marbles. There was Kimberly Ann, posing languidly before the triad of Hestia, Dione, and Aphrodite, while the background echoed once more with the unseen Ruthie's loud declarations that the whole room ought to be shipped immediately back to Greece. Revisiting such scenes proved painful for Hiawatha, for more than one reason. He asked Lady Elevenish if they might, as Tig had suggested, speed up the tape. Lady Lucy obliged, and the group was seen exiting the Museum like the Keystone Cops during a chase; a moment later, Hiawatha yelled out.

"Stop!"

Lady Elevenish froze the image.

"Why have you stopped here?" wondered Tig aloud.

"That's Sir John Soane's Museum," replied Hi, turning to look at Sarah and Mame. "You aren't allowed to tape in there. I distinctly remember you asking, Mame, and they told you no."

"Well," said Mame sheepishly, "I couldn't resist. It was so beautiful. So since they let me carry my camera, I just left it on and took my chances."

Mame had not been wrong in her assessment of the beauty of the Soane House, located only a few blocks from The British Museum, at Lincoln's Inn Fields. Most historians would agree that Sir John Soane was an architect of true and rare genius, practicing a highly personal, infinitely captivating style of construction during a long career which coincided with and helped to characterize the latter third of the Georgian era. And the house he designed for himself, subsequently opened as a public museum, was unquestionably the masterpiece of this unique architectural visionary and the artist's most enduring legacy to the London he loved. To visit the interior of the house was to enter the mind of the man who conceived it, and, as with Brunelleschi's Pazzi Chapel in Florence or Borromini's little church of San Carlo in Rome, inside, one more than beheld—one experienced, deeply and somewhat disconcertedly—the architect's own intangible but world-altering imagination at work.

Now the image frozen on the oversized television screen was of the large, well-lit parlor to the right of the entryway. In the corners of the room, where the Pompeian red walls meet the ceiling, are the prototypical convex mirrors for which the architect was famous. Antigone was studying one of these when Lady Lucy resumed playing the tape. Now it was Tig's turn to shout out.

"Stop!" she said. "What's going on there?"

"Where do you mean?" asked a puzzled Hi. "That's Ruthie, glaring at the guide."

"No, I mean what's going on behind her, in the mirror?"

Everyone, including Lady Elevenish, approached the screen, the size and resolution of which rendered it possible to make out the figures in the foyer of the house, reflected in the mirror of the adjoining room.

And in the curved glass a woman could be seen, bending over and rummaging through a rucksack.

"That's Kimberly Ann," said Hiawatha. "Lucy, if you can, slow down the machine."

Lucy, without knowing quite what all the fuss was about, was nevertheless still happy to be of service to her lover. The frames now advanced at a much decreased pace.

"And that's Ruthie's rucksack she's going through!" said Mame excitedly.

All five watched as the ghostly image of the late Kimberly Ann clearly lifted one after another of the contents of Ruthie Slatt's rucksack, pausing to read the details of what looked distinctly like a prescription bottle. Then she hastily stuffed everything back in the bag, as the camera swooped unconsciously away. The next image was a long shot of the Camford Downs from inside the little white bus.

"But what was she doing?" asked Sarah, expressing her bewilderment.

"Maybe she was looking for the money," suggested Mame.

"I think we can say that, at the very least, Kimberly Ann was getting to know a lot about Ruthie Slatt," Antigone replied, then added, "Such a learning instinct."

"Uh oh," said Sarah, "the next scene is the bad one."

"You mean—" said Hi.

"That's right," nodded Mame, and at the same moment there was a knock at Lady Lucy's door. As she was still working the controls, she called out to whoever it was to come in, and there stood Feathers.

"Superintendent Greene, M'Lady," said the butler, in a tone so soft and low that it seemed likely these words would be his last.

Hiawatha, in a flash of resolution, asked Lady Lucy if it was possible to erase part of the tape. Lucy pointed to one of perhaps forty buttons on the remote control wand.

"Good," said Hi decisively, in a newfound, husband-like tone. "You go stall Detective Greene. I'll take care of things here."

Accepting this mission with pride, and more in love than ever, Lady Elevenish made her way swiftly and silently down to distract the police chief, she didn't know exactly what from, while Hiawatha, with the tacit approval of his sister and under the grateful eyes of Sarah and Mame, pushed the button, effectively destroying the next several minutes of the recording, so that now, after a period of static following several expansive shots of the landscape surrounding Lostlindens, the viewer was treated to a close-up of Tony Trefthven-Woooser's face, explaining to Millie Dumont and Coral Marsden the antiquity of his family name. Which discourse, the reader will no doubt recall, marked the beginning of that first fateful meal in the magnificent banqueting saloon, back when all the students were still alive, and their secrets unrevealed.

XIII

THE CRYPT

*(Wherein remarkable incongruities
and coincidences are revealed)*

IT WAS TWO O'CLOCK IN THE AFTERNOON. HAVING
finished their lunch in the banqueting saloon, the
guests at Lostlindens had been informed by Inspector Greene, a louder and less amiable presence at this
meal than at dinner the night before, that the meeting he had scheduled to take place immediately afterward was to be postponed for several hours. With an
admonition to them all to reappear in the Chinese
sitting room at four o'clock, the detective made his
way, panting heavily and no doubt due to the weight
he had just put on, from the room, with two officers
in tow and, presumably, Mame Freeline's videotape
on his person. A few minutes later, Hiawatha and

Antigone found themselves in the library with Lady Elevenish and several of the students. Hiawatha was leafing through a hand-colored seventeenth-century atlas, according to the bookplate, once the property of a Lady Lavinia Scrope, whose crest was the most complex Hi had ever seen, consisting of a bell, a quiver with arrows, a snake being devoured by a bigger snake, a stag's head, what looked like a family of three cockroaches or beetles, a human eye, and a rampant goat, the whole superscribed by the Latin phrase, *simplex et suavis*, which Hi translated as "plain and pleasant." He had the sinking feeling that the murders of his two pupils were as paradoxical as this juxtaposition of word and image, the clues thus far as incompatible as these strange and rather irritating symbols.

"Oh I give up," he said at last, closing the book.

Before even Lady Elevenish could express an interest in what Hi was talking about, Mrs. Shant appeared in the doorway. Sure enough, she was still wearing her rubber gloves, which, with her large red nose and the general shortness and stoutness of her figure, made her the very image of an impromptu performer in a circus or pantomime. Whenever they saw her, the students, among whom she had become an instant favorite for the liberality with which she dispensed snacks and beverages, half expected her to pull a live rabbit from her cleavage, or an ostrich egg from behind her ear. Now, she restricted herself to making a little curtsey, indicating by this that she was not habituated to presenting herself in the public rooms of the house. Lady Elevenish, for one, was surprised to see her there.

"Yes, Mrs. Shant?" she said, hoping that there was no trouble in the kitchen.

"Yes, M'Lady," began Mrs. Shant haltingly. "It's about Feathers, M'm. 'E's quite upset about something. Quite put out, to be sure. Yelling and swearing to beat all, and nearly knocked Dither down, as I saw with my own eyes."

This was certainly news. Feathers expressing human emotions was something Lady Elevenish could not resist. And since there seemed little likelihood of getting Hi alone at the moment, Lucy announced dramatically to her somewhat disinterested companions that she must rescue her maid from her butler. In a moment she was gone, though Mrs. Shant remained behind.

Hi was reaching for another book from an upper shelf, and Tig, seated in an armchair nearby, was gazing thoughtfully into space, when suddenly Hiawatha changed his mind.

"I've got an idea," he said, quietly, so as not to distract the four or five students, including Michael Teller and Sarah Magister, who were sitting in armchairs and reading or chatting. "Let's go to the old church. We can easily walk there and back in two hours."

As he said this, Hiawatha was looking at Mrs. Shant, who still hovered awkwardly in the doorway. He wasn't sure if she was waiting for Lucy's return, or what. Still, he decided to use her to bolster his suggestion.

"Isn't that right, Mrs. Shant?" continued Hi in a loud whisper, approaching the woman. "Couldn't we get to the old church and back in under two hours?"

"You most certainly could, sir," said the lady, smiling, and when Hi turned to hear Antigone's response, Mrs. Shant suddenly turned and was gone.

"But Hi," said Tig, noticing but not knowing what to think of the cook's lingering and then her abrupt departure, "it looks awfully windy outside. What about your cold?"

"It's practically gone. Besides, I've got some warm things to wear. Come on, come on, you know it will be interesting."

Tig didn't want to discourage this slight shift toward greater enthusiasm in her brother, so she decided that they might just as well take the walk he proposed. Upon leaving the house through the kitchen garden, fragrant with flowering lavender and thyme, they were surprised to see how rapidly the weather was changing, the air becoming cooler, the sky increasingly heavy with clouds. Hiawatha, perhaps anticipating a resurgence of his cold, was wearing a dark red cardigan of Sir Manfred's, and wrapped around his neck was a Burberry scarf, a gift from Lady Elevenish. Antigone, in a yellow knit blouse and blue jeans, teased her brother, saying he looked every bit the lord of the manor.

"Or should I say, 'Lawd of the Mahnoor'?" she laughed, as they came within yards of the ancient church door.

"Say 'Load of the Manure' for all I care," Hiawatha laughed back, without even a hint of irascibility, as though the further he went from the house, the more relaxed he became.

The little parish church of Saints Filbert and Floribund, long since deconsecrated, was now a complete ruin. The restorative influence of Lady Elevenish's money had not yet reached that far from the main house, though the church was only three-quarters of a mile or so away and clearly visible from most of the rooms ranged along the southern, or garden, front. From there, the small, squat structure appeared as a boat abandoned at sea: after waging a struggle against the elements for nearly seven centuries, it seemed finally to have surrendered, ready at any moment to capsize or sink utterly under the waves of wild vegetation which engulfed it. As Hiawatha and Antigone approached the antiquated edifice, striking out from the gravel path that ran inexorably past it in the direction of the more secure and secular sanctuary of Lostlindens, both recognized what Hi identified aloud as its pronounced anthropomorphism, a human pathos suggested not only by its diminutive scale, its isolated and vulnerable situation, and its wary, crouching posture, like that of a child long accustomed to physical rebukes, but by various details of its crumbling decoration as well. The abraded facade, of a yellowish grey stone the texture and hue of which reminded Tig of the cracked and pallid complexions of sickly, chain-smoking old men, was pierced above by two darkened lancets, wholly devoid of tracery, that seemed as a result to stare lifelessly, but also in astonishment, away from the great house, at nothing. And the low doorway, its carved tympanum and triple rung of voussoirs eroded by time to an indecipherable blur, formed an inscrutable hollow, like the mouth of a stroke victim attempting, but now beyond hope of, coherent communication. For a moment, the face of the ruined building put Hiawatha horribly in mind of the gaping features of the dead Ruthie Slatt.

"I thought rotting old buildings were supposed to be romantic, evocative, spiritually uplifting," said Hi, with a hint of dread in his voice. It had been his idea to come, and now he was having his usual second thoughts.

"You've been reading too much Wordsworth," replied Tig, trying to coax her brother out of his apprehension. She had, as we have seen, initially and quite characteristically questioned the usefulness of visiting this lonely spot, but once on their way, she began to hope against all odds that they might discover something the police had overlooked.

Brother and sister stopped just short of the building, taking a moment to study its facade, which seemed, at close range, to totter slightly in the crisping breeze. Flanking the arched doorway were two badly-eroded, headless statues representing the titular saints, Filbert and Floribund. Worn almost to shadows, their primary attributes—Filbert's flowering dagger and Floribund's pear-leaf crown—were all that time had left them; aside from these, and despite the difference in sex, they were altogether indistinguishable.

"What a pity," said Antigone, expressing her own and Hiawatha's reaction to the obliterating activity of time. "It's such a pretty little place, too."

"Yes," said Hi regretfully, thinking to himself what nice souvenirs these decapitated figures would make, if only they would fit in his suitcase. "I wish we could get inside. I'm surprised not to find one of Greene's minions guarding the spot. I noticed that there's no glass in the windows on the sides of the chapel, but they're rather high up. I don't think you should be scaling the walls in your condition. Should I try to climb in and open the door?"

"That won't be necessary," said Tig, smiling and removing a key from her pocket, which she held out to Hi. "Ta-da."

"Where on earth did you get that?" said Hi in a mixture of amazement and admiration.

"Mrs. Shant gave it to me while I was in the kitchen, waiting for you to put on your costume," explained Tig. "She said she heard us talking about going to the chapel and thought we might like to see the inside."

"What a woman!" Hi exclaimed, appreciating as deeply as did his pupils a creature who was not only a great cook, but also a sort of genie when it came to personal requests.

Hiawatha turned the large key in the rusty lock, half expecting the entire building to crumble at this first contact. The door at least proved very solid, shaped like an enormous tombstone and heavy as though it were made of marble. There was of course a prodigious creak as it turned on its hinges. Daylight cut a slow and tentative path across the broad, uneven flagstones of the empty nave, and Hi and Tig, with equal slowness, followed it in.

"Well," said Hi, "I expected it to be gloomy. It's not so bad."

Antigone was more positively impressed. After the excesses of the Lostlindens interiors, here was something simple and solid to rest her mind upon. To be sure, the nave was plain even to austerity. The roof, now partially gone, was supported by six fat columns of undecorated stone which divided the entire space into three bays, with almost impassably narrow aisles flanking a wider central zone. A rotten scrap of old rug lay across the two steps that marked the dais at the eastern end; the small altar in the center of this raised area was really no more than a block of weathered limestone with the image of a cross-bearing lamb crudely gouged out of the front. And to the right of the altar, at the base of the stairs, a large wooden door opened out of the floor. The whole place smelled oddly sweet, as of burnt wood and beeswax and what one might optimistically imagine to be ancient bones comfortably relaxing into dust.

"That must be the crypt," said Hiawatha. He was pointing to the opening in the floor, but made no movement in that direction. "Should we have a look?"

"I think we should," replied Tig, though the thought of actually descending to the burial chamber was really no more appealing to her than it was to her brother. But she knew from experience that the two of them together could manage a visit which neither would probably have undertaken alone.

"It may not be possible," began Hi, nevertheless moving with his sister toward the hole. "For instance, the stairs may be gone, rotted away, perhaps. And it's bound to be too dark to see anything."

Both of these objections were overruled by a closer inspection of the opening, where they found a small iron staircase spiraling perhaps twelve feet down to a floor mottled with pale lights. Hiawatha led the way, his sister's arm on his shoulder, more for his comfort than for her support. When they reached the bottom of the stairs, they saw that a row of small quatrefoil windows high in the walls rendered the lower level almost as bright as the main church above. But whereas the upper storey, for all its dampness and lack of decoration, had seemed a small if not intimate space, the chamber below was alive with richly-sculptured surfaces and appeared to extend over a considerable area, the edges and corners of which dissolved in shadow. A great many stocky columns with foliate capitals gave the crypt the appearance of a windless, timeless grove, and interspersed among the trunks were numerous tombs, some marked by brasses or reliefs set into the floor, a few raised up and surmounted by effigies carved in stone. The overall effect was spooky, but also enchanting.

When their eyes had adjusted to the slight change in illumination, Hiawatha and Antigone began to grope more confidently among the low pillars and sarcophagi. Most of these showed signs of the same deterioration that characterized the general condition of the church's exterior and structure. Like the rubbed vines and tendrils on the capitals, the once-bright outlines on many of the brasses seemed to have been erased, the features on the effigies to have melted into their marble or alabaster skulls. All of which made for a tactile feast—there are few infinitives more delightful to the living hand or more comforting to the mortal mind than to stroke the time-softened but enduring contours of the human body in ancient stone. As Hiawatha knelt to trace the anguine lettering on the brass memorial to the fifteenth-century Sir Crispin Bothwick, named, as far as Hi could make out, after the saint on whose feast day the Battle of Agincourt claimed his father's life, Antigone sat down to rest at the base of a buxom female figure, whose expansive farthingale and lace ruff marked her as of the Elizabethan period. Tig's fingers idly caressed the little dog curled up forever at his mistress's feet.

"This one looks like Mrs. Flangas," she said, enjoying the touch of the cool stone. "Don't you agree?"

"You mean our French teacher from high school?" said Hi in response, standing up to join his sister. "Yes, I see what you mean. Except she doesn't have a mole on her chin, like Madame. Don't you remember?"

"Oh yes, I remember, the mole so huge you said she might as well decorate it with fruit stickers. She didn't like you much, did she?"

"And vice-versa. She never once taught us pronunciation. Did she even speak the language?" said Hi, staggered in retrospect at the inadequacy of his early education.

Tig didn't respond, because something had distracted her.

"What's that?" she said, pointing to the corner of the crypt furthest from the spiral stair, about twenty feet from where brother and sister were now seated, Hi with his posterior overlapping the face of his former French teacher's medieval, albeit mole-less, double.

Something incongruous, something obviously not of the place, caught in the momentary light of the changeable afternoon, flashed metallically against the dim background. The gleam seemed to emanate from the upper torso of a full-length recumbent effigy, a life-size carving which, to judge from this distance, was comparatively well-preserved. When

they approached it, it flashed again. Without knowing why, Tig and Hi felt a strange suspense, and they
moved forward slowly, as though walking barefoot
over a bathroom floor scattered with broken glass.
In a moment they were standing beside the tomb,
stunned into silence.

From the vestments he was wearing, it was clear
that the effigy represented a clergyman, possibly,
given the remains of what might have been a mitre on
his head, a bishop. His hair and beard, his gloves with
heavy rings over the fingers, and his jeweled slippers,
were all meticulously carved in cream-colored stone.
In the crook of one arm he held a staff or crosier, and
in the opposite hand he clutched a paten—or was it,
as Hiawatha instantly considered, a mirror? But it
was not the carving of the figure, nor any detail of
its original iconography, that struck Hi and his sister
dumb. Rather, the source of the reflective gleam which
had caught Tig's eye, which continued to glisten and
fade with the sunlight sifting erratically through the
clouds and the glazed quatrefoil high in the far wall,
was a thick silver wire wound twice around the stone
throat of the prelate, imitating the manner of Kimberly Ann Crestview's murder.

"But what on earth—?" gasped Hiawatha, reaching mechanically to touch the strange neckpiece,
which was spotted with rusty stains.

"No, Hi! We shouldn't touch it," Antigone exclaimed. "I think that might be blood on the wire. The police would kill you."

Hiawatha drew back slightly.

"But how did it get here? And WHY is it here? And how could the police have missed it, if, as Greene said, they already examined this area?" Hi was absolutely mystified, but also more focused and alert than he had been since the murders were discovered.

"Well," said Tig thoughtfully, "perhaps they didn't come down here at all, or if they did, maybe they weren't very thorough. You know, if it hadn't been for the light at this time of day, coming directly through that window, I might never have noticed it either. And there's also the possibility, of course, that it was put here after the police had come and gone."

As Antigone phrased this last theory, the sun again broke through the distant pane. This time Hiawatha followed the shaft with his eyes, through the dusty air, over the bright, spotted wire which sent back most of the light and made of the cleric's neck an aureole, as though a too-large halo had slipped over his head like a noose. What was left formed a small crescent moon across an otherwise invisible corner where the floor met the wall. Hiawatha walked to this spot.

"And what's this?" he found himself echoing his sister's earlier question. Bending down, he picked up what looked like a small scrap of paper, which proved in fact to be a railway ticket.

"A train ticket. Half of a return-fare, London to Camford," said Hi, reading the ticket as his sister approached. "Dated and punched for July the seventh. The same day we arrived."

Tig took the ticket and held it close to her face in order to verify, in the grey atmosphere, Hiawatha's find. After a pause, she spoke.

"I know that all of you came on the bus, with the missing driver. How did Lady Elevenish's two American friends get here?"

"They were driven from London by Dustin the chauffeur," said Hiawatha, proud to have covered that base already.

"Well, we'd better get back, and bring this ticket and news of the presumed murder weapon, to Inspector Greene. I have a feeling we'll get quite a reaction," said Tig, more pensive than ever.

"Yes, but what do you think it all means?" said Hiawatha. Then simultaneously he and his sister had the same thought, in a moment of shared, almost Siamese, consciousness. Tig expressed the idea succinctly.

"They're like coordinates on a graph," she said quietly. "The window, the wire, the railway receipt. And they point to nothing that I can see, unless it's the sky, or the dead below ground. And why, as you've said, are they here? Were we meant to find them? But we only came out on a whim!"

Tig pondered the puzzle, holding up the ticket to intercept the light. When she did this, Hiawatha noticed something.

"There's writing on the back, Tig," he said, and they both looked to see what was there. Sure enough, in a faint pencil scrawl, were three lines, apparently of poetry:

> *Love, in danger as he flies,*
> > *Drops his arrows. Envy tries*
> *To hide, but sees herself. She also dies.*

"It sounds metaphysical," said Hiawatha, though he couldn't place the poem. "Like Donne, or even Sir Manfred's beloved Crashaw."

As Hi was speaking, there was a sudden volley of soft taps, as though someone had thrown sand against the tiny windows behind them, through which the sun continued to stream at lightning intervals. They looked up and saw that it had started to rain. Tig glanced at her watch.

"Hi, it's going on four o'clock. And it's starting to pour. We'd better get back, if we don't want to be late for Mr. Greene's meeting. I think he'll be pleased with what we have to share. And this should get him off of your back, for a little while anyway."

The two of them made their way quickly up the spiral stair, leaving the trap open behind them as they had found it. Upon exiting the church, they huddled in the archway, while Hiawatha locked the door. The rain was now coming down in sheets, the wind gusting; it was small comfort to realize that, even had they remembered to bring one, an umbrella would have been of little help. With a final, sympathetic glance at the long-suffering patrons of the shrine, they headed into the torrent, moving swiftly toward the gravel drive leading up to the great house. They had gone only a few yards when they were met by Dustin, who had been sent out by Lady Elevenish to fetch them. And so, although already soaked, they were driven the half mile back to Lostlindens in Lucy's Rolls—the dark blue one, filled with a scent that Hiawatha recognized at once as Lady Lucy's favorite perfume, mixing with but still distinguishable from the stronger, more masculine odor of what was, according to his wife, Sir Manfred's preferred companion: his pipe.

XIV

EXPLANATIONS?

(Being less explanations than the
doubts attendant upon them)

THE STORM THAT TOOK HI AND TIG BY SURPRISE
proved to be only the first in a series of memorably dramatic tempests that would continue well into
the night. Like the weather, most of the occupants of
Lostlindens had become significantly gloomier than
when they had first arrived. This was visible in the
expression of despondence that each of them presented,
like ballots in a unanimous election, as they gathered in the Chinese sitting room. There, at precisely
four o'clock, while Antigone and Hiawatha were still
upstairs, hurriedly changing out of their wet clothes,
Superintendent Greene deposited his enormous bulk
upon the same ottoman he had occupied at their first
conference, and directly called them all to order.

"Ladies and gentleman," he began, in a tone which suggested great sagacity, as well as self-satisfaction, "the investigations into the deaths of Kimberly Ann Crestview and Ruthie Slatt are, insofar as you are concerned, effectively closed. The household at Lostlindens may resume its normal activities forthwith, and the rest of you are all free to depart."

This news was received with a communal gasp of astonishment, followed by uninhibited expressions of relief and contentment on the part of most of the individuals present. "It's about time," muttered Rupert Augustus, staring as usual at Paula Simon, as though their captivity had been entirely her fault. "Thank God," whispered Sarah Magister to Mame Freeline. Herman Wadkin and Paul Stripling, reaching over the pretty head of Molly Version, slapped each other's palms, as if the whole experience had been a baseball game that had gone into extra innings, to the victorious conclusion of which their own contribution had been indispensable; President Sloan would doubtless have approved the gesture. Millie Dumont and Coral Marsden didn't even wait to hear the reasons for their sudden manumission, but strode immediately out of the room to pack their things. Feathers, apparently quite his dispassionate self again after the strange disturbance of the afternoon, was white and grim, while Mrs. Shant, her nose in full bloom, seemed on the

brink of joyful tears, possibly due to the recent ingestion of a particularly strong concoction. It was at this
moment that Hiawatha and Antigone walked in.

"What's going on?" Hi asked Tony Trefthven-
Woooser, who had seemed of late to be an almost
invisible guest in the house. Now he was hovering
near the door of the room, rather furtively, or as
though ready to lead the way in the event of a fire.
Before he could respond to his colleague, Lady Elevenish sailed towards them, the large opals dangling
from her ears swept up horizontally from the speed of
her movement.

"Oh dear," said Lucy, with obviously mixed emotions but without any trace of English English in her
accent, "you're free to go. They've solved the case."

Hiawatha and Antigone exchanged meaningful
looks. But they all redirected their attention to the
police chief, who was speaking again.

"That's right. Tomorrow morning, the Americans
will be conducted by private coach to Camford. As a
personal expression of my gratitude for your coopera-
tion, I have assigned you a police escort, which will
remain with you for the last two weeks of your stay at
Woodbridge College." Then, noticing the newcomers
at the door, he interrupted himself. "Oh there you are,
Professor Musing. Mrs. Vanderlyn. I was afraid you
would miss out on the good news."

Hi and Tig were probably more surprised than any of the people around them by the inexplicable turn of events. They had not yet had an opportunity to share with the detective their recent finds, the rail ticket and the location of the silver wire that had presumably been used to murder Kimberly Ann. It was neither Hiawatha, nor Antigone, however, who spoke up first, but Michael Teller.

"I hope, Superintendent Greene, that you're going to give us some idea of what happened to our erstwhile classmates?"

Uh oh, thought Hiawatha to himself. *'Erstwhile'. Michael is clearly headed for a career in academia. Somebody ought to warn him that it isn't as wonderful as it sometimes seems. In fact, if he's learned nothing else from* English Life in Literature, *surely he's learned that.*

"Of course, my boy," replied Greene, with a most indulgent, but perhaps patronizing, smile. "To begin with, it is possible to conclude that Ruthie Slatt accidentally took her own life. I am not at liberty to go into the details now, partly in deference to her parents, who have a right to keep such details to themselves, but that she unwittingly brought about her own death is quite beyond question."

Antigone listened with intense interest. She had already formulated her own theory as to Ruthie

Slatt's demise, but she needed a little more supporting evidence. At the moment, however, she was keenly absorbed in what the detective had to say.

"As for Kimberly Ann," continued Greene, "hers is a very unfortunate case. I am afraid your bus driver, ladies and gentlemen, was an ex-convict, and a dangerous one at that. And he seems to have been involved with Miss Crestview in a rather intimate relationship. Her diary records in great detail her obsession with the man, though of course she knew nothing of his true character. For some reason yet to be determined, he killed her, and then fled. One thing seems certain, he will not be bothering any of you again. And make no mistake, we shall track him down."

"Perhaps this will be of some assistance," said Hiawatha, holding up the train ticket and approaching the police chief.

"What's that?" inquired Greene, the ebullient good humor draining so quickly from his tone that both Hi and Tig were forced to wonder if it had not been feigned. The detective stood up and snatched the ticket from the young professor.

"My sister and I," Hiawatha began courageously, but then he faltered. "My sister and I took a walk to the old parish church. There, . . ."

The Superintendent was eyeing Hiawatha with inordinate irritation—in fact, with a look of such malice that Hi stopped speaking altogether, forcing his sister to pick up where he had left off.

"There in the crypt," she began intrepidly, "we found what looked like a bloody wire around one of the tomb sculptures, and nearby, on the floor, this train ticket, which brought somebody from London to Camford on the same day the school group arrived."

Another gasp rippled like a wave over the rest of the people in the room. The students were naturally perplexed, and their anxiety renewed, by this reference to the presumed murder weapon found in the crypt. Most affected of all, however, was Inspector Greene, whose green eyes bulged in his bilious head, so that he no longer resembled Winston Churchill so much as a blood-sucking, fire-snorting frog-king from some horribly distorted fable or children's tale.

"And what," he said, hardly able to contain his anger, "what in the hell were you doing in the old chapel? You had no permission to go there!"

As usual, Lady Elevenish stepped in.

"Of course," she lied, "I gave them permission. You never indicated it was out of bounds."

Hiawatha, breathing a sigh of profound relief, felt something for her that was very much like true love.

Greene swung round to confront Lady Lucy. The two appeared well matched. But fitting opponents always make for the longest, bloodiest fights.

Hiawatha, in a sweat, tried desperately to find a way to defuse the situation, while his pupils and the members of Lady Elevenish's staff looked on in suspense and disbelief.

"Perhaps we should discuss this more privately," said Antigone at last, bewildered like her brother by the police chief's disproportionate wrath. And to think they had expected him to be pleased with their discoveries.

"There's nothing more to discuss!" shouted Greene. If he had been a more sympathetic person, both Hiawatha and Antigone would have worried for his health, watching his bloated face go from green to red. As it was, they could hardly concentrate on the words spilling furiously from his mouth, in a torrent every bit as bad as the one thundering outside. Finally, he collected himself sufficiently to conclude in a slightly calmer tone.

"All right, I think we're finished here. You may all go to your rooms. Please don't leave the house itself tonight. It will only interfere with our work. Tomorrow morning, at 10:00 AM, you will be picked up at the front entrance. I'm sure you all have packing to do, so I will say good-night. Till tomorrow morning."

With this peremptory dismissal, the group dispersed, chattering softly among themselves. Hiawatha and Antigone flanked Lady Elevenish, who bid the

Inspector a curt farewell as he silently left the room. Then Hi turned to Tig.

"What was that all about?" he asked meekly. Historically speaking, Hiawatha had a tendency to crumble instantly under any pressure exerted by a male authority figure. But in this case, he couldn't even make out exactly what the authority figure had intended to achieve.

"Oh he's just a silly old goose," said Lady Elevenish, slipping one arm through his, and, after a moment, the other through Antigone's. "I think now the best thing to do is relax. Would you two like a drink? I feel as though I could use one."

"Well, I suppose we should pack," said Hi. From the change in her expression, it was obvious that Lady Elevenish took this rather personally, and Hi was ashamed of what must have seemed his lack of gratitude, so he turned to Tig and added more brightly, "But I'm sure we have a little while before dinner, and then we can finish packing later tonight."

Tig nodded her approval, and the three of them went off toward the kitchen to find Mrs. Shant, who, it turned out, was also a wizard in the art of creating healthful, non-alcoholic beverages for conscientious mothers-to-be. Actually, Tig had rarely felt such an inclination to indulge in a stiff whisky and soda, but she decided to wait till after the murders were actually solved, for neither she nor her brother accepted for a minute the unpredictable Inspector Greene's explanation of the recent tragedies. As they sat talking in the kitchen alcove, ostensibly discussing arrangements for their departure the next day, Hiawatha and Antigone thought hard about the case, while Lady Elevenish was preoccupied with the necessity of proposing to Hiawatha her plans for prolonging his visit to Lostlindens, if only on an intermittent basis, as she was optimistic his schedule would allow.

That evening, after a buffet supper in the banqueting saloon, Lucy entertained her lover in her bedroom, dreading that it might be for the last time. Feeling uncharacteristically shy, she had not yet raised the issue of his possibly paying her nightly calls from Camford. On the marble mantelpiece, an ormolu clock shaped like a sphinx struck ten. Hiawatha, who had not even begun to pack, had arranged with his sister to meet later that night. But at the moment he was perfectly happy to be sitting on the edge of the great Madame Poisson's Polish-style bed with his hostess beside him. He was, in fact, fast coming to realize that he was fonder of Lady Elevenish than he had heretofore admitted to himself. And, among other things, the realization worried him.

"I heard him say, in the midst of all that shouting, that it was the same handwriting," Lady Elevenish softly intoned, running her fingertips over the lapels of Hiawatha's frayed but unrenounceable bathrobe, before smoothly drawing it over his shoulders.

Lucy was repeating Inspector Greene's statement concerning the writing on the railway ticket, which he thought was by the same hand that had written the note discovered in Saul Raven's room the morning after the murders: "Don't come out. I'll meet you in the empty room." She would have been pleased to know that Hiawatha was not concentrating on the recent, awkward set-to with Inspector Greene, nor on any other detail of the mystery; rather, he was studying Lucy herself, in her natural surroundings. She was, he decided, the very personification of Lostlindens, with her cool and daunting, aggressively British exterior, kept up at no little expense, surrounding a heart like her French bedroom, soft and comfortable and feminine in a most old-fashioned, even sentimental, way. A romantic with a classical facade.

"Tell me," he ventured, abruptly changing the course of the conversation, "what are you doing here?"

"What do you mean?" said Lucy, who was as glad as Hiawatha to leave off the subject of the mystery, in which she took no particular interest except for his sake, but who was at the same time afraid of being questioned on the topic of her own pretensions.

"I mean," continued Hi, "what is a woman with such talent and energy, such a capable and attractive woman, whose fearlessness in the face of fat police bullies has been proved time after time—what is such a woman, such a beautiful and accomplished woman, doing buried away in a big old country house? You should be working at the United Nations, bringing about world peace and creating a new golden age."

These, for Hiawatha, were very bold words. The truth is, she made him feel bold, and capable, and masculine, characteristics which few people would have associated with him. For her part, Lady Elevenish didn't know quite how to react to such flattery.

"Now you're being humorous," she said after a pause.

"Well," laughed Hi, helping her to remove his pyjama top over his head, without unbuttoning it. Hi could be very lazy. "I have no choice but to be humorous. My life is such a joke."

"Your life is a joke?!" Lucy responded loudly, like a cowhand yodeling after a favorite dog.

"Yes," replied Hi, a little more seriously. "It's an utter sham." And then they removed his undershirt.

"Your life is a sham?!" repeated Lucy, after the slight delay. It was as though the two of them were engaged in a contest to see who had been leading the falsest existence.

"Yes," Hi went on, tugging at his drawstring. "I mean, I'm a college professor with little or no interest in scholastic discourse, much less in the so-called academic community. What's more, I'm afraid of my students. And that's not all. If I weren't such a coward, I'd start my whole life over again, go back to school, and learn how to be honest."

Lady Elevenish loosened her own nightdress, before producing her trump card.

"My dear Hiawatha. I am from Texas."

Hiawatha wasn't sure just how adamantly he should feign incredulous surprise. He thought for a moment before responding.

"Well what does that matter? You are who you are. And the way you live doesn't really change you," he said, grasping for a metaphor, as it were, at hand, "the way clothes don't actually change your nakedness, they merely cover it. You're still naked under your clothes." And then, to illustrate the point, he sprang up and stood naked on the bed, which surprised them both. But he liked her to look at him, and she liked to oblige.

"I think I've been pretending my whole life," she went on again. "Then something about the tone of your voice, when you spoke to that poor dead girl about the boot—I can't explain it. You called me away from what I thought I was. I'm not sure I know how to be happy anymore."

Hiawatha sat down again on the bed next to Lucy.

"And Sir Manfred?" he asked, for the first time bringing up that most awkward of topics, the lady's husband. Even as he named him, Hiawatha felt a little shudder of fear run down his bare spine.

"Oh Manfred. He's worse than I am. Of course, I'm fond of him, but he hardly notices me anymore. And talk about pretentious! Manfred spent the first forty years of his life trying to prove he was a child prodigy. People got bored hearing him say he'd read *The Faerie Queene* at the age of three. And the way he said it, you'd think he'd written it. And once he discovered Crashaw, there was no reigning him in."

"Well then," said Hiawatha, "I guess we're all in the same boat." He was surprised at the note of genuine sadness in his voice.

"Yes, but what can we do about it?" Lucy asked somewhat urgently.

"Right now, I can think of only one thing to do," said Hi, grinning.

There was another long silence.

"Animal," said Lucy at last, smiling through glassy eyes.

"Beast," said Hi.

XV

A NOCTURNAL INTERLUDE

(Being the briefest chapter thus far)

ONE AFTER ANOTHER, AS THOUGH AUDITIONING for a production of King Lear, the storms broke over the Camford Downs, separated by eerie intervals of absolute calm. Even then, no moon appeared. No flying or crawling things ventured from their nests or holes. No cricket sang in the temple to Ceres, and the swans on the pond, with their heads folded under their wings, huddled together among the highest reeds and prayed for morning.

Inside the great house battered by wind and rain, the way of Libby and Saul had won out at last, at least for a surprising number of young people in the group who made up *English Life in Literature*. So, for example, Paul Stripling and Herman Wadkin shared a single bed, the lithe arms of the former wrapped protectively around the muscular torso of the latter. Strangest of all, Paula Simon, in the midst of a histrionic fit due to her unexplained abandonment by Tony Trefthven-Woooser, found unanticipated consolation in the person of Rupert Augustus, who had, as it turned out, only been waiting for an opportunity to demonstrate his long-standing devotion to her. Sarah and Mame, in separate beds, were nevertheless content to share a dream which involved them both in a narrow but definite escape. The only student without a mate was Michael Teller; but then, having taken up residence in the library, Michael's sleep might be said to have been the most restful and least lonely of all, surrounded as he was by so many voices, and importuned by them as few among the living can hope to be.

And then there was Molly Version. Molly paced the Persian carpet in her own room, smoking a cigarette, but not in frustration. It was only eleven, and she had an hour to wait for her appointment. Still standing up, she flipped through a magazine, laughing to herself whenever she thought of the strange events which had taken place in the house, all in such a short time. She was glad that her parents had insisted she remain with the group. In fact, she was sufficiently happy with the way things had turned out that she had almost forgiven her dear friends Herman and Paul for their treachery. Molly had already learned that very few people profited from grudges, and sleepless anger was bad for the skin. She stomped on her cigarette and kicked the butt under the rug. In ten more minutes she would leave.

A few doors down from Molly's room, the room in which Ruthie Slatt had met her untimely end was left exactly as her colleagues had found it, except of course that it was empty now. And directly across the hall, the wind whistled through the window next to the bed in which Kimberly Ann had breathed her last, the broken pane having been replaced for the time being with an ill-measured piece of hard plastic. If there are ghosts, then surely here was a place to find them, though it is up to the reader to judge whether or not, after death, the spirits of Kimberly Ann Crestview and Ruthie Slatt would meet on more amicable terms than those they had enjoyed in life, or whether, unheard by mortal ears, they would continue their violent conflict till another transition should transport them to a still higher, or lower, plane.

Such a thought occupied Hiawatha's mind as, just after midnight, he kissed Lady Elevenish, snoring quietly on the pillow beside him, and resumed his pyjamas and robe, before heading off to his sister's room for a thorough review of the events of the day.

XVI

WHERE LOVE LIES LOW

*(Containing a search, some danger,
and several surprises)*

W HERE DOES LOVE LIVE?"
Antigone was seated in one of the two chairs
by the window in her room with a very fat book on
her lap, her fingers marking several different places.
She wore a bright blue bathrobe over a red flannel
nightgown, and matching red slippers. Her suitcase
lay open but empty on the bed. Hiawatha, seated
opposite his sister, wasn't quite sure what she was
driving at.

"Come on, Hi, you of all people should know
where Love lives, creeping away from Lady Elevenish's rose-scented couch like Cupid slipping out on
Psyche."

"My dear little sister," said Hiawatha, still confused, "such things ought not to be talked about." He was clearly in a rare mood, to refer to Tig as his little sister, because despite the fact that Hi was nearly two years older, he usually left it to her to play the maturer role. But however he pretended to dismiss her question, his curiosity, as always, outweighed his sensitivity.

"But seriously, what are you talking about? And what are you doing carrying around such a heavy book," he teased her, turning it over to see the cover, "in your condition?" He read the title on the spine, with her fingers still stuck inside. "'*The Golden Quiver: An Anthology of English Love Poetry*'—sounds lurid— 'edited by the Reverend Mungo Thrash, M.A.'—even more lurid."

Tig passed her brother a slip of paper, on which she had copied down the three lines of verse from the back of the train ticket they had found in the crypt that afternoon. Hiawatha re-read the lines.

> *Love, in danger as he flies,*
> *Drops his arrows. Envy tries*
> *To hide, but sees herself. She also dies.*

"And what are you thinking, then?" he asked.

"What I'm thinking, Hi, is that we were meant to find that train ticket, and we were meant to believe that the person who left it there has returned to London. Or else," said Antigone with emphasis, "it's a subtler message. And so I ask you again, where does Love live?"

"Well, let me see," began Hiawatha, still a bit uncertainly. "In Shakespeare, Love's light wings help Romeo to o'er perch high walls."

Antigone was instantly on to this response, at once playful but unyielding.

"Hi, that doesn't tell us where he LIVES. Or where he might take refuge."

"Yes, yes, I know. Give me a minute," said Hi, then adding, a little more brightly, "Okay, according to Yeats, Love paces upon the mountains overhead, and hides his face amid a crowd of stars."

"Exactly!" said Tig. "He's always up high. The highest thing. For example," and she flipped open the book, "look here, in Tennyson, Love inhabits the most distant celestial sphere."

"But," continued Hi, "in Browning, Love haunts the house."

"Even better," said Tig, with unusual warmth, especially given that they were talking about poetry, for which the pretty biochemist was happy to admit no predilection. "You see, Hi, I think that there's someone with a vital connection to this case, possibly even a witness or the murderer himself—or herself—and this person, who might or might not be the same person who wrote those lines, is still in the house. In the highest storey, the attic or whatever the top floor is called in English country mansions."

"But Tig, the police must have looked up there."

"Yes, but how thoroughly? It must be quite extensive. And is that the same police who did such a marvelous job examining the crypt? Or guarding it? And I'll tell you something else. I think Mrs. Shant, much as I love her, must know something about all of this. Why else would she give us a key to the church? She practically drew us a map for finding that wire."

"So you don't believe anything that the huge and horrible Inspector Greene was saying this afternoon?"

Antigone gave her brother a look, as if to say that no one with half a brain would have fallen for such a fairy tale.

"Me neither," said Hi, acquiescing. "But what can we do? We leave tomorrow morning. Assuming that you're going to stay with us for awhile, as I hope you will. In fact, as I feel it my duty to Cornelius to pressure you to do."

"No pressure necessary," Tig smiled. "I'm going with you. But as for tonight . . ."

Hi felt a wave of familiar apprehension, mingled with a more pleasurable, if less confidence-inspiring, sense of excitement. Antigone continued at a breathless pace.

"This evening, while you were busy dallying with—"
Tig was tempted to call her 'Lady Malpronounce,' but
felt this would sound unwarrantably cross, not to mention unkind, "—with Lady Elevenish, I drummed up a
flashlight, thanks again to the infinitely accommodat-
ing Mrs. Shant. I also did a little investigating, and there
are at least three separate and easily accessed entries to
the attic area of this house. One, interestingly, is opposite the door to Lady Lucy's suite. Don't worry, I didn't
stop to listen. Another, near your room, goes to the servants' wing; I opened the unlocked door, and the stair
rises up through two floors. Finally, there's an entrance
off the kitchen—that one's locked. I couldn't very well
ask Mrs. Shant if they were all connected, but I'm willing to bet they are."

Hiawatha lightly scratched the spot on his head
where the blond hair was thinnest, a habit which
invariably signified a desire for more time to consider
his options.

"And your plan, of course, is that we should have
a look. Right now. That is to say, at twenty minutes
past midnight, in the middle of a thunderstorm, in a
house that was clearly haunted long before we arrived
to swell the number of the wakeful dead already in
residence."

"That is correct," said Tig, rising from her chair.
"We can take turns holding the flashlight."

"But are you serious?" He knew that she was, just as she knew he would come with her despite any justifiable doubts he might have as to the wisdom of the undertaking.

Tig was already leaving the room, so Hi had to chase after her to catch up. When they were side by side again, they continued to talk in a whisper.

"Now," began Tig, "since there's still an officer waiting at the end of your hallway, I suggest we at least begin with the door near Lady Lucy's room. I take it she was fast asleep when you left her?"

"Yes, poor thing, I think we've all tired her out." Hi himself looked a bit wan when he said this.

"Speak for yourself," said Tig, as they headed toward Lucy's rooms. They found the door, as Tig had predetermined, unlocked. They opened it without making a sound.

"There's a light switch," Hi happily observed. "Shall we use it? Or is your heart set on doing this in the dark?"

Tig flipped the switch by way of response, and they ascended the wooden stair. At the top, they were confronted in either direction by a continuous corridor, so long it seemed very likely that it must traverse the entire house. The floors, walls, and ceiling of this corridor had been whitewashed, which gave it, in the bluish light of the old-fashioned, regularly-spaced sconces running from one end to the other, the stark appearance of a Scandinavian interior, a passageway in some stately but provincial Danish hunting lodge or seasonal hotel.

"Which way should we go first?" asked Hi, like Hercules at the Crossroads, with no particular inclination in either direction.

"Well, unless I'm badly mistaken, the door at the end of the hallway leading right opens onto a stairwell and the servants' quarters. They must extend over the kitchen spaces, also entered through the locked door I mentioned. So we should start by going left, then doubling back and climbing that second stair to the next level."

Antigone clearly had a mental plan of the house and its division into wings and storeys, whereas Hiawatha, not a spatial thinker, already had the sensation of being a mouse in a maze.

"Can we at least agree not to break down any locked doors?" said Hi, at his sister's reference to one. "I'm really not anxious to come upon the first Lady Elevenish, chained to a newel post and foaming at the mouth, or gnawing on her own forearm because the maids forgot to feed her."

"Good heavens, Hi!" responded Tig, appreciating the image. "I would have thought that another Lady

Elevenish would only increase your prospects for future amusement."

"Hmmm" grunted Hi, as they headed left, Tig pausing at the first of several doors. Turning the handle, she found it open. Again, there was a light switch inside. Once illuminated, the room proved to be little more than a shallow closet, probably considered by earlier generations of owners an adequate place to quarter a servant; now the cell was neatly packed with cardboard boxes. The next door revealed a similar diminutive space, this one filled with linens carefully folded on deep shelves. The next was stacked high with trunks and suitcases. And so on, up and down the hall.

"Well there's hardly room for anyone in any of these," said Tig, closing the last door on the corridor, which contained an impressive collection of old and empty wine bottles, in the midst of which was suspended a fat spider, apparently for some time the sole beneficiary of all those smaller creatures attracted by the sweet smell.

"I feel like we're being so nosey," said Hi, who was nevertheless thoroughly enjoying the process of opening the doors and discovering the contents of the closets.

"Hiawatha," said Antigone, without the least hint of remorse, "this is no time to give up the very reasonable and potentially rewarding habits of a life-time." It was true that Hi was, as a rule, far nosier than his sister. "Now let's go to the servants' wing."

Again, they found the door to the servants' wing unlocked. Here, the floor was carpeted, the paint and fixtures far more modern than in the corridor they had just left. Tig stopped, apparently to listen, before whispering to Hiawatha.

"Obviously we can't try these doors. Clearly the rooms are inhabited, doubtless by Mrs. Shant, the butler, and the maids. I suggest that we go up to the next floor right away, as quietly as possible."

Hi nodded his agreement, and they made their way soundlessly to the next, presumably uppermost, level of the enormous house. At the top of the narrow stair was a small landing, and from this spot the only way forward was through an unpainted door. Passing over the threshold, they found themselves in the true attic, that is to say, under the exposed rafters supporting the leads of the roof. There was no sign that electricity was available at this height, so Antigone turned on the flashlight, casting its beam deep into the gloom that extended over an immeasurable distance broken up by ominous and dramatic shapes, like monumental sculptures waiting to be assembled into an abstract revision of Rodin's *Gates of Hell*. These, upon inspection, turned out to be more shadow than substance, a collection of large but innocuous and, for the most part, obsolete, household furnishings and accessories, including a pair of matching elephantine armoires, a badly rusted, claw-footed Victorian bathtub, a stringless harp, two or three overstuffed or completely unstuffed settees, rotting travel trunks, tall bundles of metal piping, a colossal contraption for heating water, and a hundred other lesser odds and ends. Over them all, like a tent sheltering a bazaar, the roof spread its ancient wooden canopy.

"But Tig, you can't seriously believe there's someone hiding up here!" Hi wanted to go back to bed.

The two of them had stopped, neither inclined to move further over the possibly unstable floorboards coated with a layer of cold gray dust that seemed as thick and as yielding as moss underfoot. Antigone was directing the flashlight on one after another in a row of huge round windows which, when viewed from the exterior of the house, formed the crowning feature of its primary facade. Eleven in all, each of these apertures—of a type known as *l'oeil de boeuf,* often employed by baroque architects such as Sir Christopher Wren—was approximately five feet in diameter. Tig stopped suddenly in the middle of this serial illumination.

"Hi," she said softly, "do you notice anything unusual about these windows?" And she played the light over them again, beginning with the one furthest from where they stood.

"Not especially," responded her brother, a bit disinterestedly. But then something did strike him as odd. Ten of the windows were glazed with rain, which continued to pelt them and catch the light from the torch. But on the surface of the first window there was no pattern of raindrops reflecting the light. Clearly, the glass in that window was not exposed to the weather outside.

"Let's go have a look," said Tig.

Together they walked toward the distant opening which, when they stood before it, turned out to be as they surmised—not a true window at all, but a false one, on the other side of which was apparently a wall.

"I can't imagine a wall there," continued Antigone.

"Let's open it," said Hi, twisting a small piece of wood, like a latch, on the left side. Sure enough, the window swung out smoothly. Tig, with a growing sense of conviction, impatiently pushed against the inner wall, but nothing happened.

"Shoot," she said.

"Wait a second," said Hi. He felt along the dusty boards, where they met the outer frame or sill of the false window. Suddenly there was a sharp click, and a section of the wall, the same size and shape as the great glass eye they had just pulled open, shifted inward, and the brother and sister were faced with a short passage ending in yet another stairway, this one very steep, comprising at most seven or eight treads, at the top of which was another door.

"Give me the flashlight," said Hi. "I'll go in first. Hold my hand, so you don't get lost."

"Right," said Antigone, pleased to provide her brother with this small comfort.

One after another, the siblings stepped over the round sill, both feeling strangely that in doing so they were somehow stretching and possibly breaking their ties to the safety of the main house. Perhaps this was only because, on the other side of the false window, they could no longer be sure that anyone in the inhabited quarters below would hear them, however loudly they might yell. At this moment, in any case, they made no noise, standing perfectly still at the bottom of the little stair. And their own stillness no doubt exaggerated the unambiguous sound of a board creaking somewhere overhead.

"What was that?" whispered Hiawatha, betraying more than a little nervousness.

"I think it came from beyond the door," said Antigone.

"What should we do?" he asked, but the question was more or less rhetorical. He for one was paralyzed by the possibility of proceeding further.

Tig squeezed her brother's hand.

"We'll never be satisfied if we don't see what's on the other side of that door," she said, seeming to inhale or synthesize her courage from out of the musty air. "I say we go up now."

Together they proceeded up the steps and pushed open the door. On the other side was a room, about as large as a comfortably-proportioned sleeping chamber. The analogy was suggested by the presence, on the floor against one wall, of a mattress, complete with crumpled sheets and blanket. This was the first thing that Hi's flashlight settled on, as he and Tig cautiously hovered inside the doorway. Then he redirected the beam toward the far wall, after a moment alighting on something that caused both of them to gasp aloud.

In a corner, under the cobwebs, crouched a human body, in an improbable, seemingly lifeless pose, like an abandoned marionette. Suddenly, as though someone still higher above them had twitched invisible strings, the figure was on its feet, revealing itself to be a young man—tall, gaunt, frightened, with pale eyes deeply set but dilated—in torn clothes which gave him the look of a menial servant from the nineteenth-century, a chimney sweep or some such lowly, itinerant youth, who had climbed up into the attic a hundred years ago and then been utterly forgotten. Or, to provide a better parallel of the visual incongruity suggested by his appearance, spotlit and sharply silhouetted against the mottled subfusc of crumbling plaster, it was as though a rag-tag beggar from the foreground of a painting by Caravaggio had popped up as an unexpected visitor in a spotted foyer by Vuillard. Gangly, sharp-featured, and very pale, the young man seemed to be about twenty years old. And in his hand he held a knife, awkwardly, with the long blade pointed straight out from his waist, almost as though it had been forced through him from behind.

Tig and Hi were transfixed, but the former was, for some reason, unafraid.

"Who are you?" she asked in a loud and urgent whisper.

There was an echo of other footsteps coming closer in the dark. The young man lunged forward, leaving the beam that Hiawatha had frozen upon him. Suddenly Hi was knocked down sideways, the flashlight clattering across the wooden floor.

"Tig," he moaned.

Antigone, sick with fear, frantically groped her way through the dark to retrieve the torch, which flickered and went out before she reached it.

"Hi," she yelled desperately, and as though furious. Hi drew himself up with surprising speed.

"I'm all right," he said, his voice quavering. "But we've got to get back down, before he seals us in!"

In a moment they had recovered the flashlight and were racing back down the stairs. As they hastily climbed through the oculus, they were greeted by a familiar voice, the accent unmistakably that of the second biggest state.

"Hiawatha?" called out Lady Elevenish, using her own flashlight to slice through the shadows.

Before Hi could answer her, she called out again, in even greater surprise.

"Simon?!"

"Mum?!" said a strange voice.

"Hi!" said Tig, upon whom something staggering had obviously dawned.

"Lucy?" called out Hi.

"Lucy!" repeated another, more peremptory— or, in any case, less interrogative—voice, soon to be revealed as that of Sir Manfred Elevenish.

And so they surprised or supported one another in the dark, this troupe of strange personifications of human relationships: brother and sister, lover and beloved, husband and wife and even, apparently, mother and child. They were like actors after the final curtain has fallen, waiting to hear an indication

from the audience as to whether or not their presence
onstage would be required for further appreciation.
The only actual movement was that of the light, those
in possession of a torch continuing to shift the rays
from face to face, the erratic bouncing of the shafts a
silent but eloquent illustration of the mutual disbelief
and stupefaction affecting them all. Finally, as though
these five individuals had been detected in the vio-
lation of a law concerning the maximum confusion
allowable in any private situation, several policemen
arrived, with their own flashlights, the better to arrest
and bear witness to so potentially explosive, so obviously climactic, a scene.

XVII

ENLIGHTENMENT

*(Wherein reunited characters are
required to explain themselves)*

OF COURSE, I'M NOT HIS REAL MOTHER. BUT HE DID used to call me 'Mum'."

Lady Elevenish sat in the most comfortable chair in her favorite room, directly beneath the portrait of the romping aristocrat she so strikingly resembled, or, to put it perhaps more accurately, who had so strikingly come to resemble her. It was two o'clock in the morning. Her Ladyship was, at the moment, the focal point of a number of people, like the central, much-solicited figure in a conversation piece by Pietro Longhi. On her left, with her hand resting gently on his arm, sat the thin young man whose presence in the house had been a secret till an hour ago. On her right, leaning back into the corner of a small sofa, Hiawatha held a cold washcloth to his cheek, which had been badly bruised in the fall. Next to Hiawatha, Antigone was more alert than ever. Opposite the brother and sister, Sir Manfred Elevenish, himself a large middle-aged man with a gruff and impatient way of speaking and even of looking, shared the matching sofa with Inspector Greene, in shirtsleeves and without a tie; the two of them were wedged so tightly together into the seat that it was hard to believe that either would be able to extricate himself without a dramatic, and perhaps dangerous, effort on both their parts. Behind them stood Mrs. Shant, in a pink fleece bathrobe which made her look more than ever like a pantomime Mother Goose, except that now her eyes were ringed and red. Feathers, still fully dressed, hovered behind her, and behind them all were scattered four young policemen in uniform, completing the group. Miraculously, none of the students had been roused by the commotion, or at least none had come down to investigate what was going on. No doubt they were busy amusing themselves, thought Hiawatha, though he dreaded to imagine how.

"That's right," said Sir Manfred, and all eyes turned to him. "Having no children, my wife and I raised this young man as our own."

"Well, I'm waiting for an explanation," said Inspector Greene, looking hard in the direction of

Simon Lang, who was, though no one in the room would recognize him, that same, seemingly homeless boy whom Ruthie had brought back to Bloomsbury on the second evening of the course.

After a little pause, Simon Lang spoke.

"You'd better tell them, Aunt Amy." When he said this, he looked up at Mrs. Shant. Hiawatha and Antigone were not the only ones surprised at the sound of Simon's voice, which was at odds with his appearance. He was clearly a cultivated, or at least educated, young man, his diction remarkably similar to that of the well-bred Sir Manfred.

"Well Mrs. Shant?" said the detective to the cook, as he uncomfortably craned his neck to find her. That lady moved forward into the room.

"Yes, I do know the tale," she began in a whimper, "and it's as sad a one as I hope you may ever come to 'ear, but not uncommon after all. This boy is the child of my miscreant sister, Serena Lang. May I be struck down for judging her, but it's the truth. She used to work 'ere with me in the kitchens, over twenty years ago, under the then 'ead cook, Mrs. Blackball, in the late Lady Bothwick's time. Serena was never up to any good, and she got herself with child, this 'ere Simon being the issue. When the little boy was five, she went from Lostlindens—I was told it would be temporary—and left the little boy with me. Not long after, the new owners came. I hid the boy as long as I could, not wanting to risk my own and his positions. But Lady Elevenish, God bless 'er—" at this point, Lucy sniffled, and so did Mrs. Shant, "—found out the truth. And not only did they not send him away, but they sort of adopted him, Her Ladyship and Sir Manfred. And that is 'ow he came to live at Lostlindens as one of the family, so to speak, till he got to be fourteen or thereabouts, when up and out of the blue his wretched mother comes and takes him back."

There was a little intermission in Mrs. Shant's testimony. Hiawatha, at this point suspicious of everybody, wanted to ask why Mrs. Shant dropped only some of her 'h's, but clearly such a question was not a priority. Antigone, too, had a number of questions, but held them inside till the story was brought to a close.

"You see," said the cook, holding her hands together over her stomach like a woman praying, "Serena wanted money from Sir Manfred. And though they were willing to give it, Lady Elevenish feared that the boy would someday accuse them of trying to buy him. Especially under the evil influence of Serena, though she still is my sister."

"And how is it you find yourself here now, Mr. Lang?" said Inspector Greene, once again giving the impression that he already knew the answer to the question he had asked. At the same time, he did not sound aggressive or even angry when he spoke.

Simon Lang looked to Lucy, who squeezed his arm and dabbed at her eyes with a handkerchief. He swiped a tear starting from his own eye before responding to the police chief.

"Well, sir, I came here because of Ruthie. She was a friend I made in London, where I've been living for some time, since leaving my mother in Newcastle."

"Why, oh why didn't you come back to us?" Lucy broke in, with a harrowing shudder in her voice, which most of the others immediately felt.

Simon looked at her sadly.

"It was too late. I had already gotten into trouble. Big trouble," he said, ominously. Then he went on.

"So anyway, Ruthie and I hit it off. I was sleeping rough at the time. She tried to put me up in the hotel where her school group was staying. The first night it wasn't possible because of her roommate, but a couple of nights later, it turned out the girl found someone else to room with, and so Ruthie and I had a room to ourselves. We got involved."

"Idyllic," interrupted Greene, but again, with considerably less force than Hi and Tig knew him to have at his command. "And you also got *her* involved, didn't you?"

Simon squirmed visibly, but didn't reply at once.

"Yes sir," he said at last, and then, eyeing quickly and successively every individual in the room, he announced, like an alcoholic at his first AA meeting, "You see, I'm what's known as a fence."

Though she wasn't exactly sure what her adoptive son meant by the term, Lady Lucy winced. Hi and Tig silently nodded, as both of them had immediately identified, from their wide reading in nineteenth-century fiction, something Dickensian about the young man.

"Well, you're really more a courier than a fence," said Inspector Greene. "But do go on. Tell us all what you were doing here."

"Wait!" Lady Lucy interjected, turning to her husband. "Shouldn't we get him a lawyer?"

When you came right down to it, thought Hiawatha admiringly, nobody was as quick on the draw as Lucy.

"It's all right, Mum," said Simon, and then he resumed his account. "Well, at one point, Ruthie told me that the group was scheduled to stay at a big country house near Camford. Imagine my surprise. She wanted me to come with her. I didn't tell her my whole story, but I can't deny I was curious to see the house again. It was, after all, the only place I've ever felt at home. But then we got a really big idea. You see, I was due to go on an important job—"

"Drugs?" asked one of the young police officers lurking in the background.

"Fountain pens," said Simon. "Hundreds of them, top-of the line, Cartier, Mont Blanc, some solid gold, all untraceable, but very hot. Worth well over a hundred thousand on the market. Anyway, I was to deliver the goods to the dealer and collect forty-thousand pounds. But Ruthie and I—I mean, I—decided to keep the money, hide out with Ruthie at the old homestead, and then go with her when she went back to the States. It would have been my last job."

"It was, my boy, it was," said Greene, at once avuncular and foreboding. Lady Elevenish glared at him through teary eyes.

"I gave Ruthie the money to hold. Then I took the train down from London. Had a happy but secret homecoming with Aunt Amy."

Mrs. Shant had come to rest in a chair on the periphery of the room. Now she looked up and smiled vaguely.

"Anyway," continued Simon, "it was a tense situation for me and Ruthie. I had already explained that the thieves whose money it rightfully was—in a manner of speaking—would be pretty angry when I turned up missing. I didn't know yet just how angry. But I had to lie low. I was hiding out near the old chapel, long after dark, when I saw somebody making his way up the drive. I recognized him as a new guy working for my boss. He must have followed me from London. He might even have found out about Ruthie, who she was or at least what she looked like. I was in a panic. I took a chance by sneaking up to the house and sending a note through the window which I knew was hers, telling her not to come out, as prearranged, but instead to meet me in the empty room, meaning, as I had described beforehand, an old playroom under the staircase in the hall, which was sure to be deserted. You see, although I was able to find out in advance which room was Ruthie's, her regular roommate had apparently been having some difficulty with her boyfriend, so that she might actually be hanging around, and we couldn't be too careful. Just after I'd tossed the note, however, Ruthie caught up with me on the gravel drive. She'd been watching for me from the hall window and told me that there'd been a change of plans, that she had gotten her own room, a gift from Kimberly Ann, and that I should meet her there instead. I started to warn her about the guy from London, but she said she'd already taken precautions. I didn't know what she meant, but at the time it seemed safer to get her back into the house."

"So, you knew Kimberly Ann, eh?" interrupted Detective Greene.

"I knew of her, and naturally I was suspicious when I heard that she'd given her room to Ruthie. Ruthie was suspicious, too. You see, they hated one another."

"Oh really?" said a voice from the doorway. It was Tony Trefthven-Woooser, who had heard noises earlier in the evening, and, despite a newfound shyness resulting from the discovery of his affair with Paula Simon, had finally decided to come down, if only to convey the fact that he was on his own. He was wearing a very expensive bathrobe, and the sarcasm of his question made it clear that he was regaining at least a little of his usual self-confidence.

"But how did the note wind up in my room? I mean Saul Raven's room, where I was?" he asked. He had apparently been listening for some time.

"I think I know," said Hi. "If the Inspector will allow?"

Greene made a gesture of invitation. Hi, still holding the cloth to his face, went on.

"Kimberly Ann, newly-installed at her own insistence in Ruthie's old room, found the note, and assumed, like many of us, that the empty room must either be Libby's or Saul's, since those two were always together. So, obsessed as she was with her unworthy rival, she went to see what was waiting for Ruthie, no doubt dropping the note when she found there was no one in Saul's room. Or perhaps, seeing Tony asleep inside, she dropped it in surprise."

"Excellent," said Greene. "I couldn't have done better myself."

Lady Elevenish looked proudly at Hi, who looked warily at Sir Manfred, who stared impatiently off into space, like a man waiting to be summoned by the dental hygienist.

"But I still don't see how Ruthie was killed," said Hi.

"I told you before," said Inspector Greene, "she killed herself. Accidentally."

At this, Antigone guffawed.

"But maybe your sister has a better idea," Greene went on, good-naturedly, turning to her.

In fact, she did.

"Well, I can't explain it all," she began modestly, "but I think there can be little doubt that Kimberly Ann poisoned her. As I understand from my brother, Ruthie was taking a generic form of Prozac. We saw on Mame Freeline's videotape that Kimberly Ann was aware of this."

"Ah yes, the videotape, missing some bits," said Inspector Greene, which made Hi blush. But Tig went right on talking.

"The mixing of even the most common, over-the-counter drugs with mood inhibitors such as Prozac can prove fatal, as any first-year chemistry student can tell you. And Kimberly Ann had been a first-year chemistry student twice. So, if I am asked to guess what happened, I would say that Kimberly Ann crumbled up some drug that she knew would combine fatally with Ruthie's prescription, say an easily obtained appetite suppressant of some sort, using it to coat one or more pieces of marzipan which she left for the unsuspecting victim on the bedside table. What this other drug was, I can't be sure —"

While Tig was speaking, Simon Lang's jaw had dropped, and he became increasingly agitated.

"It was this," he said, taking from his pocket a little piece of hard plastic of the sort in which certain types of pills are dispensed, the capsules removed by pressing them through small transparent bubbles. "I found it in Ruthie's backpack when I discovered she was dead," said Simon, handing the packet to Tig. "They're diet pills, but Ruthie wasn't on a diet. And she told me herself that Kimberly Ann had recently offered her a diet pill as a typical joke, but that it was even crueller than Kimberly Ann knew, because Ruthie's doctor had specifically warned her about the dangers of mixing anything with what she was already taking."

"But how on earth can you say for sure that Kimberly Ann killed her, if, as you've just said, you found these pills in Ruthie's backpack?" This question came from Tony. "I admit, everything points to her, but—"

"The evidence is perhaps circumstantial," said Tig, examining the pills, "but think about it. The bedroom exchange, at Kimberly Ann's suggestion. The marzipan on the night stand. From what I've been told, Ruthie had quite an appetite, and Kimberly Ann was counting on her not being able to resist a snack, especially as she had been escorted somewhat prematurely from the dinner table several hours earlier. What's more, you'd need very little of this to do the job, once you removed the powder from the capsules. She probably pressed it into two or three pieces of candy. Then, if Ruthie ate them, she'd be dead, but if someone else ate any, nothing would happen."

"She did it. I saw her do it. She did it and then she tried to make it look like Ruthie stupidly killed herself."

Up to this point, Simon Lang had spoken in a clear and dispassionate manner, like a student reciting lines or an essay he had learned for a speech class. But now, his tone and bearing changed dramatically, the rhythm of his sentences became broken, his delivery more breathless and emotional.

"What do you mean, you saw her do it?" asked Greene with interest.

"I mean, when I came up to meet Ruthie in her new room, shortly after two, I saw Kimberly Ann coming out. I was confused, of course, and immediately hid myself. When I was sure she was gone, I went into the room, and that's when I found Ruthie. Dead." And here he faltered. "I was wild. I didn't know what to think. I admit I looked in her rucksack, to see if the money was gone, because that would suggest that the guy from London had gotten hold of her. But what I found, at the very top, were these pills. Then I heard some muffled noises coming from across the hall. I opened the door a crack, and saw the man I told you about, leaving the room I had just seen Kimberly Ann go into. I was petrified. After half an hour or so, I finally got up the nerve to creep out and look into the other room. There was Ruthie's name still on the door, and inside, sprawling across the bed, that horrible girl, with a wire around her neck. The thug must have mistaken her for Ruthie and then killed her when she denied any knowledge of the money. Or maybe out of spite. Anyway, I arranged her on the bed. I hated her, but I covered her up. I took the wire, I can't say why. I was in a kind of trance, thinking over and over to myself, she got what she deserved. Then I found this little mirror on the dresser, and stuck it in her hand, as a sort of sign, an accusation."

"'Envy tries to hide, but sees herself. She also dies,'" quoted Tig.

"Exactly," said Simon. "I took the pills with me, but I left the money behind, partly because I was afraid of being caught with it. But you see, it was never the money that mattered, it was only Ruthie. Then I realized, I had no place to go. The London men must still be looking for me. And I knew now how serious they were. It was risky, but I decided to hide right here."

"You should have come to me!" cried Lucy.

"I wanted to. Really I did. I thought, if I could get the police to go away, then I might be able to let you in on it. So I had the idea of trying to make people think that whoever might have killed Kimberly Ann was long gone, probably back to London. I decided to arrange something in the chapel, it being close by, but not too close."

"Your Aunt Shant providing you with food the whole time?" inquired the Superintendent.

Mrs. Shant looked worried, perhaps, but by no means ashamed.

"I did 'elp him, as he was family. Though I'd've done as much for a dog. But I wanted him to turn himself in."

"Anyway," said Greene, "go on."

"Well," Simon spoke calmly again, "I wanted to turn myself in, too, mainly because I felt I couldn't just leave with everyone thinking Ruthie had killed herself."

"And you were still being hunted," the Inspector reminded him.

Simon nodded. "So, since I knew my way around here as well as anybody, I set myself up in the attic, and after the situation cooled down a bit, I left the bloody wire around the sculpture in the crypt, and nearby, the ticket, with the lines of poetry I made up, as much as to say: 'I'm here, but I'm gone.' In fact, I sort of hoped my mother—I mean you"—here Simon glanced up at Lucy Elevenish, who clearly suffered another in a series of unenviable pangs, "might recognize the writing as mine. Then you'd know I was nearby. But I was so ashamed, and I didn't really want to get caught. I felt torn like that, you see. I wanted someone to find me, but at the same time, I was afraid."

"Poetry?" said Sir Manfred, who seemed to come alive at the mention of the only thing that really interested him.

"That's correct, Sir Manfred," said Greene, "your adopted son is a poet." The detective took the train ticket from his pocket and handed it to his neighbor, who lifted his silver-rimmed spectacles higher on his nose in order to scrutinize it.

Hiawatha piped up suddenly.

"So all that stuff you told us about Kimberly Ann being killed by the bus driver, and the case being solved, was a ploy?"

"My dear Professor Musing," replied Greene, "you and your sister were not the only people investigating this case. The police had already found the wire in the chapel. And also the ticket, rather pointedly hinting that we should go looking in London. Well, I decided that if someone was so obviously trying to tell us something, we would pretend not to hear it, thereby forcing them to speak louder, if you see my point. So we deliberately left the wire and the ticket where we came upon them. That's why I was so furious when you and Antigone—I beg your pardon, I mean of course, you, Professor Musing—does that ever become confusing?—publicized your discovery this afternoon. For which I tender my apologies now."

Hiawatha and Antigone nodded simultaneously, not so much to show they forgave the detective's earlier brusqueness as to indicate that he should go on.

"So, leaving the chapel clues in place, as a sort of challenge to this unknown player, we decided to break up the gathering at the house. With regard to the Americans, we had already concluded that you were all innocent, based on the glaring naiveté that is your greatest charm as a race."

Here, Greene smiled, and Hi sneered.

"That still left a number of people. The driver, the cook, Feathers the butler. Mr. Cadwallader the gardener even had a son who had come from London to

Camford that day, so the train ticket might have been his. It is, after all, a commuter line, a punched ticket would not have been hard to get hold of, nor could it be considered conclusive. But the message it conveyed was clearly to get us away from the house. So that's what we pretended to do. Close the case, and send everybody off, keeping an eye on you, of course, for your own protection. Since the bus driver had already run away—we assumed, because he was afraid of what Ruthie's father would do to him after she turned up dead—we made him the temporary scapegoat, as a way of justifying our letting you all go."

"And the story of Kimberly Ann's affair with MacMenzies, described in her diary. That was made up too?" Tig pondered aloud.

"Not entirely, Professor Musing. Kimberly Ann was in fact obsessed with MacMenzies, recording as much in her journal. But it's very unlikely anything physical took place. You see, as Ruthie's secret body-guard, MacMenzies kept a close watch over her, and this attention, the reason for which was unknown to Kimberly Ann, seems to have driven her mad."

"And where is MacMenzies now?" asked Hi. He wasn't altogether satisfied with the inspector's reading of the bus driver as clue.

"Dead," replied Greene. "In London. His body, or what was left of it, turned up by the Embankment and is now in the Charing Cross morgue. How or why he died remains a mystery, but if I were to speculate, I would say that he followed the men, whom he no doubt believed to have killed Ruthie, to London. Bill Slatt seems fairly certain that he would have done that. But when he caught up with them, he found out he'd bitten off more than he could chew. Anyway, the police in London are looking into it and have a few leads."

"And it's this poem that led you to Simon?" asked Sir Manfred, in the critical tone of a scholar who finds a loophole in a rival's theory.

"Not me," said Greene with a laugh. "That was entirely due to the ingenuity of the Musings. We had searched the house fairly thoroughly but were no match for Mr. Lang. Of course, we continued to keep an eye on the place. And so, Sir Manfred, when your taxi turned in at the gate after midnight, bringing you unexpectedly home, naturally my men followed you in. I was contacted, and we all converged."

"It's certainly ironic," said Hiawatha to no one in particular. "Ruthie Slatt was killed by a diet pill she never knew she was eating."

"And Kimberly Ann died being mistaken for the woman she had just killed," said Antigone, puzzled not by the facts, but by the insolubly mysterious motivations for most human actions.

"And now, I think, it is time to leave."

With great difficulty, and no assistance from Sir Manfred, Greene worked his way out of the settee. Then he signaled to his men, and they moved behind Simon Lang, who rose up with Lady Elevenish beside him. She was still holding the prodigal's hand.

"Don't worry, Lady Elevenish, we'll take good care of him," said the Inspector.

Lucy hugged him once, then looked away. After a moment, she sat down again, and put her hand out. Hiawatha took it almost automatically. Antigone rested her own hand on her brother's arm. Mrs. Shant sniffled again, while Feathers remained absolutely still. Just before he was out of the room, Simon turned around.

"It wasn't for the money," he said, passionately and pathetically. "It was for Ruthie."

Then, with the policemen, he was gone.

"You know," said Sir Manfred, after a lengthy pause of which he himself seemed barely aware, "these lines don't scan properly. I might have expected better from Simon."

XVIII

THE EFFECTS OF ENLIGHTENMENT

(Especially on Hiawatha)

B ACK IN ANTIGONE'S ROOM, SHE AND HIAWATHA
faced each other from their usual seats in front of
the window. Moments ago they had said good-night
to Sir Manfred and Lady Lucy in the great hallway
below. Both brother and sister had been conscious of a
chilling politeness, certainly of nobody's choosing, but
thrust upon them by the unexpected return of their
hostess's husband. The physical introduction of a new
character, however vividly that individual may have
been present all along in the imaginations of those
persons who have established separate relationships
among themselves—and there can be little doubt that
Sir Manfred occasionally loomed large in the thoughts

of Hiawatha Musing, not to mention those of his lover and his sister—inevitably brings about a review of attitudes and an adjustment of tone. If this is generally true among acquaintances, it is invariable and absolute among people involved in clandestine romance, and is recommended as well for members of their families, if they are more than mere disinterested bystanders, as Antigone certainly was.

Perhaps aware of this dictum, the rain had changed its tactics, too. Now, instead of attacking the house with a steady battery of droplets, it seemed to have gathered up and reorganized its forces, charging less regularly but more intensely, so that all of a sudden a sound of banging would arise, as though spectral visitors were running from door to window to roof to door, knocking to be let in, which, thanks to Lady Lucy's renovations, they never were. After a particularly severe pummeling of this sort, Antigone spoke.

"Poor Hi," she said softly, studying his damaged cheekbone. "But it does give you a violent and distinguished look, like a buccaneer."

"Better a buccaneer than a bookworm, I suppose," said Hiawatha.

There was a considerable pause, before he spoke again.

"You know, Tig, I'm still not sure I accept it all."

"Well," said his sister, "if you're talking about what happened to Ruthie and Kimberly Ann, there are alternative interpretations. For example, it may yet turn out that there was no 'thug', that Simon Lang invented him, or that he existed only in the kid's mind. When he found Ruthie dead, he himself crossed the hall and killed Kimberly Ann. He took the wire with him because he'd brought it in. And then he was tortured by remorse."

"But there must have been someone else out there, as he said, what with the money, and MacMenzies dead."

"Yes, it may turn out that way. Or it may be that MacMenzies WAS that other person."

Hi seemed already to have anticipated his sister's train of thought.

"That crossed my mind, too. This 'new guy working for my boss' that Simon claimed to have seen could have been the bus driver, a convicted criminal who, in the course of watching Ruthie, might have found out about the money. In fact, she told Simon she'd taken precautions—she might even have told MacMenzies about their plan. And then he himself came looking for the cash, and when he got to Ruthie's room, he couldn't find it. What he did find was Kimberly Ann. He either panicked and killed her, or—once again—she was mistaken, in the dark, for her archenemy. And then, Bill Slatt had HIM killed." Hi seemed to think this was quite plausible, given his own brief encounter with Ruthie's father.

"The bus driver sounds to me like the kind of person who could get himself killed all on his own."

"And Kimberly Ann was a murderer," Hi continued. "For some reason, it should be harder to believe."

"It sounds as though her mother knew. Poor Mrs. Frink," said Tig sympathetically.

"And all the Slatts," said her brother in the same tone. Then he added, "Strange how and why people do things."

"I was thinking the same thing," said Tig.

"Of course you were," said her brother, smiling.

"Now, what about you?" said Tig.

The smile left Hi's face. He was feeling curiously angry, but at whom?

"What do you mean?" he said.

"I mean, where will you go from here?"

"We're going to Camford," said Hi, "and you're coming too."

"I didn't mean that."

There was another protracted pause, during which Antigone tried to assess her brother's mood. No doubt he was disappointed in many ways, as who, in the same position, would not be? She could at least try to console him.

"You know, Hi, I think people always expect experience to work for them, to show them what's what. Like those troughs that miners use to separate the gold from the less valuable ores and silt. But that seems to me problematic. I mean, as often as not, we learn very little from experience, be it traumatic, such as having two of your students die on a trip abroad, or . . . romantic."

Here Antigone stopped, out of respect for the delicacy of the situation. When her brother didn't respond, she went on.

"And then we all make the same mistake, thinking we can go back and retrieve the beautiful, or at least the useful part of experience. But that's not true. In the end, you're always left with the same, inseparable sediment, glittering in certain lights, but mainly dross, after all."

Hiawatha was only half listening to his sister's increasingly heartfelt attempt to comfort him. It was, in fact, a strange moment of role reversal for the two of them, Tig waxing unostentatiously poetic, and Hi, preoccupied with his worried, loveless existence, quietly analytic.

He had been pressured into supervising this course, he thought to himself. He had never wanted to come. For that matter, he had not particularly wanted to go with Tig up into the attic this evening, but of course everything his sister had supposed had proved correct. And Lady Elevenish? She had picked him up like a trinket from a tray at a Fortnum and Mason's sale. And now he was forced to admit he was fond, weaker in the long run than even he found it pleasurable to be. Putty, in a word. Everything seemed out of his hands. Hi had thought it would be so easy to say good-bye. Now he would probably be deprived of the opportunity. Served him right. He was angry at himself.

"I thought that solutions were supposed to make one happy," he said at last, and as much to himself as to his sister. "I thought they were somehow the goal."

The puzzled expression on Hiawatha Musing's face made him seem younger, reminded Antigone of the way he had looked when he first left home to go to college, a period which figured large in her own life because it was the first time she had been separated from her older brother. She felt a sudden need to muster a maturer, scientific self to respond to him now, to bring things back into focus.

"I'm a scientist. Every solution creates more problems. Welcome to my world."

When Hi said nothing, she spoke again.

"We'd better get to bed. The students will be up and needing you before you know it."

"I find it hard to believe that you know the word dross, but not the word buddle," said Hi, standing up as the clock chimed four.

"What?" said Tig.

"Buddle," said Hi. "That's the word for the trough the miners use."

"Yes, I suppose it would be," said Tig, somehow relieved.

EPILOGUE

(Being the epilogue)

S O THAT'S THAT," SAID LADY ELEVENISH, STANDING next to her husband in the great hall at Lostlindens. Expensively dressed and meticulously groomed, the two of them presented a reflexive image of comfort, of common tendencies and ways of thinking and even—and this was Lucy's greatest triumph, after all—of a shared past, of a private heritage that predated and would outlast their own limited lives. For many, this a-temporal but organic oneness is the primary function of marriage. Its expression, both deliberate and accidental, is what allows us, with only visual evidence to go on and without knowing the deeper connections and disconnections which are the true test of any case, to recognize people as "together"—as belonging to a pair, a couple, for good or ill, whether it be to the general satisfaction or eternal disappointment of the parties concerned. At this moment, Sir Manfred and Lady Lucy bore all the outward signs of having been set apart for each other before the world began. Though they did not touch, their forms nevertheless seemed tangential in a way which suggested that neither could remain upright in the absence of the other. If Hiawatha had been there, he would have felt this, would in fact have acknowledged the mutual calling into being of the two figures, and he would undoubtedly have been struck by their balance and counterpoint, as though (to borrow one last analogy from the history of art), the famous Arnolfini couple had returned to the Van Eyck studio many years later, to have their portrait made again, perhaps as an anniversary image, to prove that whatever they had been or done to one another over the intervening decades, the original picture had undeniably recorded a marriage in every sense of the word.

"Yes, that's very heartening," said Sir Manfred, closing the vitrine. "We must invite that ass from the V & A back as soon as possible, eh, my dear?"

They were looking into the case at a large but badly fraying piece of blackened leather the general outline of which suggested, like the silhouette of Italy excerpted from the broader geography of Europe, the lower section of a human leg. After the recent disorganization of the household resulting from the visit of the American students and the investigation into the violent deaths of two of them, Sir Manfred had decided to carry out a thorough and long-overdue cleaning of the mansion's attic storey, during which this object had been discovered in an old limewood box hidden under a floorboard beneath Simon's Lang's temporary, makeshift bed. Pinned to the leather was a piece of paper, with a single line in faded, nineteenth-century script:

The real boot, which Wilfrid threatened to sell.

"Good old Aunt Lydia," said Sir Manfred for the tenth time since the object had turned up. "She was always trying to rescue things from her brothers, both of whom would have pawned her, too, if it would have brought them any money to expand their gambling debts. Fortunately for her she was too plain to profit from."

"Well, we'd better be going," said Lady Lucy thoughtfully.

"Yes, yes," said her husband, a tiny bit brusquely, fishing his pipe out of his jacket pocket. They were due at the local magistrate's office at noon, in order to present a formal plea with regard to the future of their erstwhile dependent, the young Mr. Lang. Despite the unpromising circumstances which had brought Simon back to them, it was becoming increasingly likely that he would not have to go to prison, but would be released into the probationary custody of his former unofficial guardians. With this end in view, Lucy had thrown herself into the project, bringing to it all the vigor that had marked her orchestration of Sir Manfred's knighthood. One of the reasons for this was obvious, namely, the deep affection she bore the young man whose spiritual mother at least she felt herself to be. But another reason was that she was desperately trying to distract herself from another love, for quite another young man.

Since the unanticipated return of Lucy's husband, she had not seen Hiawatha Musing alone. In fact, she had not seen him at all since the morning of his departure in the company of his sister and the surviving members of *English Life in Literature*. Not that she hadn't tried. She had called the dormitory at Woodbridge College, where the class was staying, on several occasions, but each time she had been told that Professor Musing was out. Finally she had sent a message to arrange an afternoon meeting for tea. Hearing nothing in reply, Lucy hopefully arrived at the hour and place she had appointed. Hiawatha never appeared. He was, as she correctly assumed, hiding, partly out of shame but also—and she knew him well enough to make this accurate deduction as well—out of fear that their association might represent a potentially disastrous risk for her. And the fact remained that Lucy was more adamantly resolved than ever not to lose her English life, and Lostlindens in particular, a house to which, however much she had invested in it, her husband had at least as strong a claim. So she wisely accepted her lover's scruples, and thought no less of him for his cowardice, rather more highly of him for his sensitivity to her own.

During the two weeks following their release from Lostlindens, the despondence of Hiawatha and his students, like the clouds over Camford where they were staying, lifted and returned but eventually gave in again to a fine summer. While it would be wrong to say that the group immediately recovered from the tragic affair at the country house, it was not long after they left it that they re-found their bearings and their capacity for enjoyment. They started over, as it were, and with a renewed energy, throwing themselves, like Lady Elevenish into the rescue of Simon Lang, into both their scholastic and their extracurricular pursuits, almost in defiance of the pall of disharmony and malice that in retrospect must be said to have threatened them since the earliest days of the course. Their newfound fervor was perhaps also, to some small extent, a parting gesture to their deceased peers, nostalgic anecdotes about whom were heard and tolerated with increasing frequency, as memories of the actual subjects became blurred.

Supervising, if not always leading, the students in this revival of activity was Hiawatha, with the collaborative assistance of Tony Trefthven-Woooser, the latter now relieved, by Rupert Augustus, of the burdensome expectations of Paula Simon. They were accompanied by Antigone, who fast became a favorite with the group. Once again, as in London, *English Life in Literature* filled its days with more or less educational visits and events. Like a band of mountebanks tracking down rumors of gullible towns, they raced from stately home to collegiate archive, from museum to restaurant to concert hall. They picnicked on the Camford Downs, where Herman Wadkin tried unsuccessfully to push over one of the famous cows. They spent a morning at Blenheim, where Saul and Libby got themselves locked into a single bathroom stall. They punted on the River Tine, known colloquially as the "Prong," one of three small tributaries of the Thames converging to form a fork-like configuration which is the only notable feature of the local topography.

In short, things gradually returned to normal, and it is perhaps best to leave them that way, offering this slightly distant view of the English countryside as a concession to those who look for symmetry in a story. Though perhaps it will be equally acceptable to follow the American students back to their own country, for at the same moment that Lady Lucy and Sir Manfred were locking up their priceless article of Shakespearean attire, the plane carrying *English Life in Literature* touched down in Illinois. Not all of *English Life in Literature*, of course. Kimberly Ann Crestview and Ruthie Slatt had taken earlier flights, from separate airports; by now they were long underground. Their former colleagues, however, had never felt more vitally optimistic, experiencing that sensation of profound confidence in an almost tangible future that is the inevitable, if only momentary, reaction to the successful conclusion of a transatlantic flight. Even Hiawatha, waking from another bad dream in which each of his pupils was armed and irritable, considered proudly that he had at least succeeded in bringing most of them home alive. Antigone, who was coming to stay with her brother in Chicago, where they would shortly be joined by her husband Cornelius, studied each of the students for the last time. One by one they stood up, stretching, then walking a little stiffly down the carpeted aisles to their parents and friends at the gate.

Molly Version, the last to deplane due to a mild but in the end futile flirtation with one of the air stewards, smiled brightly, as though expecting to be greeted by photographers. She bore a secret of which even she herself was not yet aware, pregnant as she would soon prove to be, though God alone knew for certain whether Dustin, the chauffeur, or Feathers, the butler, did it.